THE BLACKSTONE BEAR

ALSO BY ALICIA MONTGOMERY

THE TRUE MATES SERIES

Fated Mates

Blood Moon

Romancing the Alpha

Witch's Mate

Taming the Beast

Tempted by the Wolf

THE LONE WOLF DEFENDERS SERIES

Killian's Secret

Loving Quinn

All for Connor

ABOUT THE AUTHOR

Alicia Montgomery has always dreamed of becoming a romance novel writer. She started writing down her stories in now long-forgotten diaries and notebooks, never thinking that her dream would come true. After taking the well-worn path to a stable career, she is now plunging into the world of self-publishing.

facebook.com/aliciamontgomeryauthor
twitter.com/amontromance
bookbub.com/authors/alicia-montgomery

*For my mother-in-law, J.
Your strength and love inspire me everyday.
Thank you for raising my husband into the man he is today.*

This is a work of fiction. Names, characters, businesses, places, events, locales, and incidents are either the products of the author's imagination or used in a fictitious manner. Any resemblance to actual persons, living or dead, or actual events is purely coincidental.

Copyright © 2018 Alicia Montgomery
Cover design by Melody Simmons
Edited by Red Ribbon Editing

All rights reserved.

THE BLACKSTONE BEAR

BLACKSTONE MOUNTAIN BOOK 3

ALICIA MONTGOMERY

PROLOGUE

A FEW WEEKS AGO...

As Penny Bennet walked into The Den, she couldn't help but feel like it was walking into an *actual* den.

Several pairs of eyes followed her as she cut across the room, tracking her like prey. It wasn't busy, but there was a group of about six men in the corner, another group of four around a small table, and two more playing billiards. All of them had stopped what they were doing to look at her. With an audible swallow, she held her head high and continued forward.

It's not that she'd never been around shifters before. There were plenty of them back in Houston, and, having grown up just outside Blackstone, she'd known a few of them during high school. But so many of them in one small place was intimidating. The Den, and the town of Blackstone itself, was a well-known haunt for their kind. Bears, wolves, big cats, and (as she'd heard) a dragon or two—lots of them lived there. She couldn't help the sliver of fear slicing through her.

Stay calm, she told herself. *They're just shifters*. Like humans, except they could turn into animals with big teeth and claws. Anyway, if she wanted this job, she would have to get used to this.

Penny cleared her throat as she approached the bar. "E-excuse me?" she called to the figure with his back turned to her. "I-I—" She cleared her throat louder, hoping to get rid of the phlegm that seemed to have gotten stuck there. "I'm looking for Mr. Grimes."

The figure turned around. "Whaddaya need with me?" The man's thick white beard covered most of his face, and his eyebrows were drawn together into what Penny guessed was a permanent frown. He was wearing a red flannel shirt that stretched over his wide, barrel-like chest and suspenders tucked into black corduroy pants. "Who are you?"

"I'm Penny," she said with a gulp. "Penny Bennet."

His eyes lit up in recognition. "Ah, Greta's girl?" The frown on his face seemed less severe now.

She nodded. "Yeah. She's my neighbor and when I mentioned I needed a job, she said you might be looking for a waitress."

"One of my bartenders left," he said. "Got one of my waitresses, Heather, to fill in. But she's doing a good job so I'm giving her the position permanently." He leaned over, clasping his meaty hands together on the countertop. "You've waitressed before?"

"Y-yes," she said, taking a folder out of her purse. "Here's my resume—"

"A resume?" he said with a chortle, waving the folder away. "Don't need that, girl. Just tell me about you."

Light blue eyes stared back at her, and Penny had a strange feeling wash over her. She suddenly understood what 'soul-piercing' meant. Was it true what people said about shifters? Could they read your mind or tell when you're lying? She'd heard rumors and seen those conspiracy videos online from anti-shifter groups, but she'd always taken them with a grain of salt. Shifters never bothered her, so she never bothered with them.

"Well … uh, I'm originally from Greenville," she began. "And then I moved to Houston to live with my grandmother when I was sixteen." Her voice shook, and she hoped he wouldn't ask why. When he didn't, she let out a small breath of relief. "I finished high school there and well, there wasn't money for college, so I started as a hostess at this local place called Rinaldi's. It wasn't a fancy place or anything, just a nice family-run restaurant. Did that for a year and then moved to waitressing. I've been waiting tables for four years now."

"Do you have experience working in bars?"

"Oh yeah," she said. "My second job was at a sports bar downtown."

"Houston's a big city. Why are you back here?" he asked quickly.

"Grams died last year," she stated. "And then I got a call. My daddy got sick …," she trailed off, biting her lip and hoping he wouldn't ask any more questions.

"Well, sounds like you have solid experience," Mr. Grimes said. "But there's one more thing I gotta ask you: do you think you can handle the clientele around here?"

"Huh?"

"I'm not gonna mince words with ya," he said. "I keep things as orderly as I can, and no one messes with me or my people. But, a lot of these guys, they work hard over at the mines, you know? They might need to blow off steam. I can't always keep an eye on you. I need someone who can hold their own, especially when my customers are idiots."

"Oh. Mr. Grimes—"

"Tim," he corrected.

"Tim," she said. "I can handle myself." She hoped he didn't notice the tremor in her voice. "I'm a very hard worker, and I've been around a lot of rowdy customers. You should see what happens when the Rockets are playing," she said with a small laugh, trying to sound casual.

Tim's expression didn't change. "And the fact that my customers are shifters doesn't scare ya?"

"Of course not," she said confidently. *There are plenty of other things in the world to be scared of,* she added silently.

Tim paused and studied her for what seemed like a full minute. "All right then. Can you start tonight?"

"Tonight?" she squeaked.

"Yeah. I got a big party; could use the help. Unless you think you can't cut it."

She was hoping she'd have a day, but beggars couldn't be choosers. With Grams gone, so was her rent-controlled apartment in the city, and she couldn't afford the new rent on her own. She had had no choice but to move back to Greenville. Daddy had left the trailer to her when he died, but there were medical bills, plus gas, water, and electricity to pay. She couldn't rely on her savings forever. Some tip money would help with her dwindling funds. "Of course I can. Thank you so much, Mr.—I mean, Tim."

He nodded to another girl who was wiping down tables. "Olive'll sort you out with the uniform. Your jeans and shoes are fine, but you need the shirt." He called Olive over and told her to take Penny to the back. "When you're done, go ask Heather to teach you the ropes while we're not too busy."

Olive let out an exasperated sigh as her face turned sour. "C'mon, new girl, let's find you a shirt." She didn't even wait for Penny to say a word before walking away.

Penny followed Olive to the storage room in the back. When she got there, Olive was rooting around in one of the bins, then took out a dark-colored bundle.

"Sorry, we don't have shirts in your size," she said, raising a brow at Penny's bust. "This'll have to do."

"Oh ... uh, thanks," she said, feeling her face go warm. Her chest had always been a problem, in more ways than one. Olive handed her the shirt, shrugged, and left her alone.

Penny wasn't sure if she was meant to change in the storage room, but since the other girl hadn't offered to take her to a changing room, she took off her blouse and slipped the shirt on. It was definitely snug around the chest and stretched the logo a bit, but it fit. She fluffed her red curls into place and straightened her shoulders.

This isn't so bad, she told herself as she walked out. It was better than having to find work back in Greenville. She really didn't want to have to go back and face all the people in her hometown again. But with all those medical expenses, there was no money to take her anywhere else. She was stuck. But she wasn't going to feel sorry for herself.

"No siree," she said under her breath. Grams would be turning over in her grave. The old woman was a tough bird and taught Penny to suck it up. Ironically, if Grams were around, she'd be the first one to tell Penny to stop thinking about her.

Tim was gone, but now there was a blond woman cleaning

the bar top. "Hi," she said to the woman. "I'm Penny, the new waitress."

"Oh, hello Penny," the bartender said with a bright smile. She wiped her hand on her jeans and offered it to her. "I'm Heather. Nice to meet ya."

She shook it. "Tim said to come talk to you when I'm done changing."

"Right," Heather said. "Well, let me show you what you need to do and introduce you to the rest of the crew."

Heather turned out to be much more personable than Tim and nicer than Olive. When she introduced her to Olive, the other woman snapped, "We've met," then walked away.

"Sorry about Olive's bitch face," Heather said.

Penny giggled. "She's what my grams would have called a 'lemon face.'" In polite company, maybe. Grams would definitely have called Olive a bitch face.

Heather laughed. "Ha! She does look like she sucked on a lemon." She sighed. "Don't worry, she'll get over it."

"Over what?"

"Well …." Heather lowered her voice. "If you ask me, she's pretty disappointed that one of the former employees here, Catherine, snagged a Lennox."

"A what?"

"A Lennox. Particularly, Matthew Lennox."

"Who's that?" Penny asked.

"Oh, you're not from Blackstone, are you?"

She shook her head.

"Well, let me give you the short version. The Lennoxes are a family of dragons who founded Blackstone. They own the blackstone mines, and they're richer than sin," Heather said. "And Matthew's like, the head honcho of Lennox Corporation. Anyway, he met Catherine, who used to be the bartender here, and fell head over heels for her. It's a very long story but," she nodded to the banner above the bar which read *'Congratulations Matthew and Catherine,'* "tonight's their engagement party. And bitch face just can't accept that Matthew chose Catherine, especially after she's been shaking her perky little titties at him since she started here."

Penny chuckled. "Oh my. I guess I'd be bitchy-faced too if that happened to me." Though she didn't mean it, it seemed like the right thing to say.

Heather looked down at her chest. "I don't know, I think if any man saw those first …."

Penny went red.

"Don't worry, I'll order a larger size for you. Now, let me show you how to get the tab out …."

Heather was a patient teacher, and Penny was grateful for the help. It wasn't anything she hadn't done before, but the system was slightly different from the sports bar back in Houston. She knew the only way to learn was to do it, so she plunged in head first, immediately taking her first order as soon as Heather went back to slinging drinks.

After a few hours, The Den was starting to get crowded. It was a Saturday night after all. And really, it wasn't that much different than any bar anywhere else. If anything, Penny actually felt safer here, especially with Tim keeping a watchful eye over everything. Sure, a lot of the men's gazes would linger a little too long on her chest or she could feel them staring at her ass while she walked away or a couple would call her "sweetie" or "honey," but no one tried anything inappropriate. And shifters were damned good tippers. She was already skipping happily, thinking of how much she'd be taking home tonight.

As Penny was heading back to the bar to grab another

round of drinks, a cheer erupted behind her, along with the sounds of poppers and confetti guns.

"Happy couple's here," Heather said pointing to the door.

As she glanced back, she saw a man and woman surrounded by well-wishers. "Oh my." They were a beautiful couple—he was tall, dark-haired, and handsome, while the woman was willowy, slim, and gorgeous. They were like the prom king and queen striding in to greet their subjects. No wonder poor Olive was so sour.

"Need help with those?" Heather asked, looking at the full tray.

"I'm fine," she said, a bit embarrassed at being caught staring. "I'll be right back."

Penny lifted the tray and walked over to the table, dispensing the drinks easily. One of the couples at another table stopped her, and she took their orders. As she pivoted on her heels, Penny felt something very solid bump into her.

Penny braced herself for the fall and prepared for that inevitable moment when her butt would hit the floor. However, a pair of hands grabbed her arms, stopping her from tumbling over. *Oh my....* Something, no *someone*, smelled so *good*. The cologne was heady and male and fresh. As she looked up, she saw a handsome face covered with a thick beard. He was looking past her at the crowd of people. Or, rather, over her head, as the man was gigantic, especially compared to her petite frame. A small sound escaped from her as she felt her feet lift off the ground. The man had picked her up and placed her aside, then went on his merry way.

"Eeep!" She covered her mouth as soon as the squeak came out. She stared after the man, watching his large back retreating from her. A shiver ran through her, thinking of his warm, calloused palms on her bare arms. *What happened?*

She watched him join a table—not just any table, but *the* table—the one where the newly engaged couple was holding court with their friends and family. *Of course.* The man who bumped into her was hunky and gorgeous and he was one of them, the elite of Blackstone. *He didn't even look at me.* Why would he? She was just a waitress after all.

Shaking off imaginary dust from her jeans, she walked back to the bar. "Two rum and cokes and a whiskey," she said to Heather.

"You okay?" the other woman asked with a frown. "You're redder than a firetruck."

Penny touched her cheek, which was indeed warm. "I'm fine." She glanced over at the table again and saw the man laughing with his friends. It made him appear even more handsome, the way he seemed so relax and genuine.

"Oh, Ben's here," Heather said, following her gaze. "I didn't see him come in."

"Do you know him?"

"Well, not personally, but sure, everyone knows him. He's head of the mining operations and related to the Lennoxes. Cousins or something."

"Right." So, handsome, popular, *and* rich. Of course he wouldn't notice someone like her. Girls were probably throwing themselves at him all the time. Why would he notice a nobody waitress?

Penny shook her head. No use thinking about that. "You got those drinks for me?"

"Coming right up."

CHAPTER 1

Present day...

The massive blond grizzly bear charged at the tree, smashing its block head against the thick trunk. Six-inch, razor-sharp claws cut through the bark, shredding it like tissue paper. The bear reared its head back, got up on its hind legs, and growled, raising its paws in the air. Birds flew overhead, shaken from their perches by the resounding roar. With a loud thump, front paws landed on the soft forest floor.

The bear walked silently through the forest, sniffing for something. A few minutes later, a rustling sound caught its attention. Moving closer, it found its target—a young doe, ambling out from the safety of the tree line, probably hoping to find something fresh to nibble on.

The air was still and quiet. The grizzly crouched down, ready to pounce on its meal, when it reared back its head and let out a low, guttural sound. The doe started, then leapt away, disappearing into the cover of trees in the distance.

The bear let out an angry growl and rolled on its back, swatting its face with its claws until it drew blood. Slowly, the animal began to shrink, the matted fur receding into skin and muscle. The figure on the ground was now half the size of the grizzly, covered in mud and blood.

"Enough," Ben Walker snarled. A rumble from his chest made him grit his teeth. "I said that's enough." But would the monster inside him know what enough meant?

He lay in the dirt, naked as the day he was born. Deep, haggard breaths made his chest rise and fall. Looking up, he saw the light fading in the distance, and when his breathing became steady, he slowly got to his feet.

"Damn bear," he grumbled, wiping the blood from his face. The cuts were already healing, but they hurt like a sonofabitch. He circled back to where he had started shifting and retrieved his shirt, pants, socks, and boots. The chilly late winter air didn't bother him; he was a shifter after all and his body warmed and cooled as necessary. But he had to be careful as he didn't know who or what he could run into, so he put on his clothes for his trek home.

The hike back would be a couple of miles, but it would be good to tire out his body and his mind. The sleepless nights were taking a toll on him, and some days, he exhausted himself during the day just so he could get some rest at night.

If his family and friends could see him ... he slammed his fist into a nearby tree. *No, they could never know.* This was his secret to keep, and the burden would stay on him. He wished his mom and dad were around, so he could talk to them. But, he wasn't a child anymore. They had told him the truth some time ago, thinking it would make things easier. It hadn't.

It was inevitable, he supposed. The bad blood taking over. Dad never said bad blood, but Ben knew that's what he meant.

It was making his bear crazy and unmanageable. The animal inside him wanted to take control of their body. It had been happening for months. Barely controllable shifts. The physical clawing at his insides. The worst had come when he woke up covered in blood next to a young buck. The grizzly didn't even eat the thing; just ripped it to shreds. And yet ….

Ben blinked. The memory of the delicious, sweet scent was so clear in his mind it was as if it was right there. He wracked his brain, trying to figure out what it was. Fruity, maybe raspberries or oranges or a combination of both. All he knew was it somehow calmed the beast inside him. But where had he smelled it? Whenever he was out, he would always sniff the air, trying to get a whiff. He thought he was going crazy until he smelled it again a few days ago. Traces of it anyway, before it disappeared like a ghost.

A ringing sound interrupted his thoughts, and he fished his phone from his pocket. "Hello," he said in a gruff voice.

"Ben, my man," Nathan Caldwell answered back. "Dude, where the hell are you?"

"I'm at home," he answered.

"No, you're not," his friend said. "I'm outside your cabin. Been ringing the doorbell for the last ten minutes."

Shit. "I mean, I'm just out back. I've been hiking."

"Dude, in this weather?"

Ben picked up his pace. "Yeah. What do you want?"

"I'm here to pick you up. We're going out."

He rolled his eyes. "You must be getting desperate for a wing man if you're calling *me*. Are you going to hit up Luke next when I say no?"

"Ha! I want to meet girls, not scare them away. And no, I'm not calling you to be my new wingman. Unless you *are* interested."

"No," he said flatly. He could see his cabin in the distance, and he ran faster, if only so he could get rid of Nathan sooner.

"Aww, you sure? You know I never strike out. Besides, when's the last time you had some pus—"

"Nathan," he warned.

"You know, I've never seen you bring any girls home."

"Just because I don't parade a string of women around, doesn't mean I don't get any," he said. He came up behind his cabin, jogged up the steps of the wraparound porch, and made his way to the front door. "I do fine on my own."

Nathan turned to him and slipped his phone back into his jeans. "Just kidding, man. I know you got game; you're just not flashy." He frowned. "You ... okay?"

"Yeah, like I said, I was just out back ... enjoying the fresh air," he added quickly. Even without the blood on his face, he must have looked like shit. "So, what are you doing here?"

"I told you, we're going out."

"You could have just called," Ben pointed out.

"Yeah, but then you would have made some excuse to not go. C'mon man, live a little. There's, like, tons of horny human girls out tonight, looking for some fun. If you put in half as much effort as me, you could be swimming in pus—er, women." He waved his hand at Ben. "Chicks dig the beard and the lumberjack look these days."

"Not interested," he said, making a grab for the front door.

"You don't even know why we're going out. It's Jason's bachelor party, man! You can't miss that."

Ben stopped. His cousin, Jason Lennox, had just gotten engaged and the wedding was coming up soon. "I thought Jason didn't want a bachelor party?"

Nathan huffed. "So? He might not want one, but he *needs* one."

"Christina will chop off your balls if she finds out you took Jason to a strip club."

"I asked her permission, don't worry. And we're just having a boys' night at The Den. I happen to like my balls where they are, *thank you very much*," Nate said with a wince.

Ben laughed. He'd heard about what his cousin's fiancée was capable of and did not want to mess with her. "Fine. If it's for Jason."

"Good." Nathan let out a relieved sigh. "You know Matthew's on board; we only have to convince Luke."

"Oh, I gotta see how you plan to do that," Ben said. "Let me change, and we'll head over to his place."

CHAPTER 2

"Sorry, Boss," Penny said as she whipped past Tim on her way to the employee locker room. "Stupid car," she muttered unhappily as she went to her cubby. She whipped off her blouse and wiggled into her uniform shirt, not bothering to check her reflection in the mirror. Her hair was probably a mess, but she quickly ran her fingers through the curls, hoping that would be enough to tame them. She hadn't even had time to put anything more on her face than a swipe of lip gloss.

Her busted up old Toyota chose the worst time to act up. Friday night was one of the busiest nights at The Den, which meant everyone had to come in. One of the girls had given her a dirty look as she passed by on her way to the locker room, but Penny tried to ignore it. She'd been a model employee the last few weeks, yet none of the girls aside from Heather seemed to warm up to her. The vivacious bartender had told her it was probably because her 'cute face and bodacious bod' got her more tips than anyone else, but that didn't make her feel any better. She let out a deep sigh. It really shouldn't bother her, after all these years, the way most people just saw boobs and a butt when they looked at her. She couldn't help but—

"Whoops! Sorry!" She collided into someone as she was rushing out of the locker room.

"Watch it!" the other girl said, her arms going around Penny to prevent them both from falling.

Penny disentangled herself from the other girl. "What are you ... oh, are you new?"

The girl raised a brow at her as her gaze swept from head to toe. "Yeah, name's Mia," she said with a smirk that made Penny uncomfortable. Mia was tall with long dark hair that fell to her hips and lips slicked with red lipstick.

"I'm Penny. Sorry, I gotta go. My shift started an hour ago. Nice to meet ya!" she said with a wave, then quickly made her way out to the floor.

"Ooohh, girl, you chose the wrong night to be late," Heather said as she filled four glasses with seltzer water.

Penny tied an apron around her waist. "It's my damn car. Just got it back from the mechanic, too." Ugh, she couldn't afford another costly repair. She supposed she should be glad the car started at all today. If only it would hang on for another couple of weeks.

"Table six," Heather said, pointing to the table across the room and shoving a tray of drinks at her. "Olive's just about ready to have an aneurysm."

As if on cue, Olive shot Penny a nasty look from across the room as she took out a foot from her shoe and rubbed it with her palm.

"Sorry!" she mouthed to Olive. "You can tell her to take five. I'll take care of her tables." Heather gave her a two-fingered salute, then signaled the haggard-looking Olive to go on break.

Penny grabbed the tray and walked over to table six, giving the patrons a quick apology as she served them their drinks. Next, she stopped by the other tables, checking to see if they needed anything and taking more orders, then she hopped back to the bar.

Working at The Den was hard, but she was used to it. She wasn't afraid of hard work, and it was nice to be able to pay her bills and still have some extra cash left over. She could figure out what to do next once she built up her savings. As the weeks passed by, she had realized one thing: no way was she going to be stuck in Greenville. Once she had enough money, maybe she'd head back to Houston. Joan and Gary Rinaldi, her previous employers at the restaurant, told her she'd be welcome back anytime. Of course, if she needed to make another trip to the mechanic, it would set her back a bit.

After a busy first hour, that miraculous lull every server prays for finally came when all the tables had their orders filled and everyone was happy. Penny took advantage of it and stood by the bar, leaning on the counter to get the weight off her feet.

"Another one bites the dust," Heather said.

"Huh?" she asked.

"Another Lennox. Jason this time." She shook her head. "I never thought I'd see the day."

Penny turned her gaze to where Heather was looking—a table in the corner where a group of guys were laughing and drinking. "Eeep," she squeaked.

It was déjà vu. Like her first night here. They were even sitting at the same table, though this time, none of the girls were around. Matthew, Jason, and Nathan, she knew. The latter two were regulars and flirted with her a bit, but they were always nice to her and left her a good tip. The fourth guy, she didn't know, but something about him made her want to stay away. And then there was the last guy. It was him. *Ben Walker.*

After that first night, he never came back to The Den. But then she'd seen him again yesterday. She was enjoying the quiet afternoon at her favorite cafe when Christina Stavros walked in with her friends.

She still couldn't believe it. Memories of that night were enough to make her hands start shaking. She had gone out to the back to take her break and this creepy customer had followed her. He tried to grab her, and she froze, but Christina was there to save her. She didn't even get to thank Christina because she had run away.

Seeing Christina at the cafe was her chance. As it turned out, Christina was the nicest person, even offering to teach her to defend herself. But then she saw Ben walk into the cafe and she panicked and ran.

A flush crept up her neck, thinking of how close she'd been. She whipped around so Heather couldn't see her as her breath came in short bursts.

"You okay, Penny?" Heather sounded worried.

"Me? Yeah, I'm fine." *He's just a guy*, she told herself. A guy who's never looked at her and didn't even know she existed. *Deep breaths. That's it.*

"That table's mine," Olive said, as she sauntered past them and flashed Penny a pointed look. "You owe me."

"You can have them," Penny said. The moment the words were out of her mouth, she regretted them. As she watched Olive lean over and flirt with Ben, she felt an unreasonable stab of jealousy. "What?" she said out loud, then shook her head. "I must be getting a fever or something."

Penny returned to her tables, taking checks and orders back and forth from the bar. She kept her head and gaze down as she tried not to look over at their table, but she couldn't help herself and took a peek. *Hmmm.* Where was Ben? She saw the other guys—Nate, Jason, Matthew, and the tall, scary-looking one—at the table but not him. Did he leave? Or maybe he went with Olive—

"Penny? Penny Bennet?"

She whipped around at the sound of her name. "Yes?"

The man who called her name was standing with two other guys around a table, beer bottles in hand. "It is you! Penny, it's me. Kyle. Kyle Roberts."

Penny squinted her eyes. "Oh. Kyle. From Greenville High." She swallowed a gulp.

Kyle Roberts. She knew who he was. He hadn't changed much over the years, except maybe for the slight paunch around the middle and some thinning hair.

"Yeah, it's me. And you remember Jeremy and Cam," he nodded to his friends. "So, you're looking good."

That familiar, uncomfortable feeling crawled through her as Kyle's eyes ran up and down her body. She hugged the tray in her hands to her chest. "Thanks."

"I didn't know you were back in Colorado," he slurred, moving closer to her. "Or that you worked here."

"Y-y-yeah, I moved back a few weeks ago," she stammered. The stink of alcohol on his breath was unmistakable. What were her old high school classmates doing in a shifter bar? "I've been working here for a while now. I've never seen you here before." In fact, it was one of the reasons she took this job, even though it was a good twenty-minute drive from Greenville. So she wouldn't *have* to see anyone from her past.

"Yeah, well, me and the boys heard some things. Someone told us things get *wild* around here," Kyle said meaningfully. "Of course, if I had known you were here, I would have guessed it was a different kind of wild. So, tell me, how's your *momma*?" Behind him, Jeremy and Cam snickered.

"I wouldn't know; I haven't seen her in years," she said in a cold voice, then turned to walk away. Oh no, she would not be having this conversation here.

"Hey, c'mon." Kyle stepped in front of her, blocking her way. "Don't be that way."

"Kyle, I'm working," she pleaded.

"What? Just because you got out of Greenville a couple of years back, you think you're too good for us?" he said, his voice raising.

"Please, just leave me alone." She tried to side step him, but he blocked her again.

"C'mon now, pretty Penny." He stroked a finger down her bare arm. "We just want to have some fun. What time does your shift end? I'm sure me and the boys could show you a good time." He leaned down to her ear. "We know you like having a good time." His hand cupped her ass and pulled her close enough so her hip brushed the bulge growing in his pants. "Just like momma, right?"

The anger that had been brewing in her, for years maybe, suddenly reared its ugly head. She had had enough. "Fuck you, Kyle!" she yelled, pushing him away.

"You wish," Kyle said with a smirk. He stalked closer to her. "C'mon, are you shy now? You've been giving it up to everyone for years."

"No!" she cried as she evaded his grasp. "Stay away from

me!" She staggered back and bumped into one of the tables, sending it and her crashing down. As her butt painfully hit the floor, the whole room seemed to quiet down, and the air felt heavy.

Penny got to her knees and rubbed her sore behind. As she was contemplating what to do next, the sound of heavy footsteps made her look up.

It was him. Ben Walker, striding across the room toward her. He glanced briefly at her, his blue eyes blazing. She looked around, behind her, unsure. But there was no one else on the floor, so he must have been looking at her.

Kyle let out an audible gulp as Ben came closer. "Hey, what's up man?" he asked, trying to act casual. "Are you—" He didn't finish his sentence because a loud series of pops and a deafening roar rang out over the din in the room.

Penny thought she was in a dream for a moment because Ben was suddenly gone and in his place was the biggest grizzly bear she'd ever seen.

The bear reared up, raising its giants paws overhead. Screams and shouts filled the air, followed by more pops and growls. Glass shattered everywhere, and panic was thick all around her.

"Goddammit, Ben!" someone shouted.

"Take him down! Get him outta here."

Penny remained frozen in fear. Around her, she could hear people shouting. And the smell ... oh God, it smelled like a zoo. Fur, feathers, and all kinds of animal stenches reeked up the air.

"Let's go!"

Someone grabbed her by the elbow and got her to her feet, then pushed her toward the exit. When she reached the door, she took a last glance backward, her eyes going wide as she saw the gigantic grizzly. It was so tall, its head nearly touched the ceiling. A gray wolf had pounced on its back, while a tall, blond man was pushing against its side.

"Penny!"

She turned her head as she exited The Den. The fresh air cleared the stench from her nose. "Heather!" she cried as she collapsed into the other girl's arms. "What ...."

Heather grabbed onto her. "It's okay, everything should be under control now."

Sounds of loud animal growls and glass and wood shattering from inside The Den made her wince. "That's under control?"

"Yeah, well ... this doesn't happen too often," Heather said. "I mean, it is a bar and people get drunk, but Tim has a strict no-shifting policy inside."

"Then why did he ...."

"I don't know. Ben's not known to be a hothead, but you know, these guys ... sometimes things can just trigger them. Maybe he was having a bad day. Did you see anything?"

"No," she said. "I mean—"

"Penny! Heather!" Tim called as he ran to them. "You girls okay?"

They nodded.

"Good." He let out an unhappy growl. "I think Luke and the others have got things under control. I'll let you know when it's okay to go in and get your belongings."

"S-sure," Penny stammered as Tim walked back into the bar.

"He probably doesn't want to get the police involved," Heather said. "Especially since it's a shifter thing."

Penny breathed a sigh of relief. She was glad Ben wasn't

going to get into any trouble with the police. But what had triggered him?

"Penny?" Heather asked. "Are you okay?"

"Yeah," she said, putting the thoughts of shifters out her mind. "I'm good. I'm freezing though."

"Me too," Heather said with a laugh. "Look, Tim's waving at us." She pointed to their boss, who was pointing to the back of the building. "Looks like we can get our stuff from the locker room."

Good, she thought. Between getting nearly trampled by a bunch of animals and running into the people she was trying to avoid, she was ready to call it a night. A shiver ran over her as Kyle's words rang in her ear. The past hurts she had put away were now flooding back into her mind, but she pushed them deep inside again.

All she wanted right now was to go home and curl up under the covers with a good book and forget about tonight.

CHAPTER 3

BEN REMEMBERED two things from those few moments before blinding rage took over: that familiar sweet scent in the air and a flash of something red. Not blood red, but a coppery color. And soft. It had been so subtle, he hadn't even noticed it at the time. He had been walking back to their table from the john when he felt something brush against him as he walked by.

It was *her*. As her coppery curls caressed his arm, the sweet smell of oranges and raspberries went straight into his system. He turned around and realized he had walked right behind her as she stood talking to some customers. He couldn't see her face, but he stared at her, memorizing the details of her petite frame and the sensuous curves of her ass. He couldn't move; he stood rooted to the spot.

Something had rumbled in his chest, a deep sound that sounded like ….

Mi—

Before he could complete his thought, he saw that man

grab her. She obviously did not want his attention, so she struggled and fell back. Then all hell broke loose.

"What the fuck was that about, Ben?" a familiar voice asked, bringing him back to the present.

Ben's eyes flew open, and he found himself staring up at the ceiling of a log cabin. It wasn't his, he was pretty sure of that. It didn't smell like his cabin. It smelled like ….

"Luke?" he called as he got up, looking around for his cousin. He had been lying on the floor of the sparse cabin, but he wasn't alone. Nathan and Luke were seated on the leather couch, while Jason stood off to the side, pacing back and forth.

"What the hell is going on?" Jason asked, his face red with anger. Jason, his younger cousin who was always getting into trouble—the one who he more often than not had to rescue—was mad at him. And it was obvious why.

"I just … I couldn't stop." Ben ran his fingers through his hair, trying to make sense of it all. The girl. Some guy touching her. And her falling and getting hurt. "Shit."

"You mean you just went berserk for no reason?" Nathan asked. Luke stared at Ben, his eerie golden eyes piercing straight through him.

"I mean, it wasn't for no reason." How could he explain this? "Er, it was that guy. He was being an asshole."

"Human," Luke spat. "One of those townies over from Greenville. Bet he was hoping for a look-see at us shifters."

"Yeah, well looks like he got more than he bargained for," Nathan snickered.

"You almost killed him," Jason pointed out. "They took him to the hospital. He just got out of surgery. Matthew's making good with him and the authorities now."

Fuck. "And the girl?"

"What girl are you talking about?" Jason asked. "No one else was hurt, as far as we know."

"Your bear's been out of control," Luke stated.

The silence and tension in the room grew thick. How did Luke know? Did they all know? Ben stood up and looked around the room. "It's nothing," he said. "Can I borrow some clothes or something? I can walk home." He had to get out of there.

"I can take you home, man," Nathan offered. "Just sit down or something. Talk to us."

These guys weren't his brothers, but they were the closest thing he had to them. It didn't matter, though. This wasn't their burden. "I'm fine," he said through gritted teeth. "I can walk home." It was probably a couple of miles back to his cabin. He could grab his spare keys and then pick up his Jeep at The Den. *Oh fuck.* "I should probably go and apologize to Tim for destroying his bar." He could only imagine the kind of damage he had done. Plus, he could go check on the girl.

Jason shook his head and put his palm on Ben's shoulder to stop him. "No way."

"Why the hell not?"

"Tim's furious at you, doesn't want you anywhere near him or the bar." Jason tsked. "You nearly took him down, Ben."

"Fucking shit," he cursed. He couldn't believe it. Tim's polar bear was a mean sonofabitch. Probably would have been Alpha if there were more of his kind around. "Until when?"

"Until he says so," Jason said.

Dammit. How the hell was he supposed to find out who she was? He had to know if she was okay. For a second, he thought of asking Jason or Nathan—they knew almost all the staff at The Den—but he quickly shut down that idea. For some reason, he didn't want them knowing he was looking for her.

"Tell Tim I'm sorry and I'll pay for all the damages." He knew Matthew would probably try to pay for everything, but it was his responsibility. Besides, it's not like he didn't have the money. He wasn't as rich as his dragon cousins, but he did all right.

Jason let out an exasperated breath. "Fine. Luke, can you get Ben some clothes? I can drive him home."

"Thanks, man." He had to find out who she was. And for the first time in a long while, his bear did something that surprised him. It agreed with him.

The Den had been closed for two days. The cleanup and construction crew were there the day after the incident, and they worked through the weekend to get the place ready to open by Monday night. Ben knew because he'd been waiting across the street, watching all the cars and people who went in and out of the parking lot. Matthew must have brought in the crew from his grandfather's construction company, as he didn't know how else Tim could have gotten service that fast.

Tim had said Ben wasn't welcome in The Den, but he didn't say he couldn't watch from outside. After work, he borrowed one of the old trucks they used at the mines, in case anyone recognized his Jeep. He didn't want to miss his chance to run into the girl.

What if she had quit? What if she never came back? A deep growl rumbled from his chest. Yeah, even his bear wasn't happy with that thought.

"Well, who's fault is that?" he said, then shook his head. "I must be going crazy, talking to you."

He let out a deep breath and placed his hands on the steering wheel, tapping his fingers across the worn leather cover. It was an hour before opening time and there were already a couple of cars in the parking lot. He saw Tim and a few of his employees, but no sign of the girl.

He was nearly losing hope when he spotted a rusty Toyota the color of baby puke sputter into the parking lot. It was still too early for customers, and the car had out-of-state plates. It stopped in one of the employee spots, and the door opened. The petite redhead stepped out and swung her purse over her shoulder, then slammed the door shut.

That was definitely her. Even from a distance, his enhanced sight could make out the coppery red curls. And the curve of her ass that seemed to be burned in his mind. His cock twitched, and he wondered what the rest of her looked like.

He rubbed his hand over his face. No, he wasn't here for *that*. He was just going to go to her and say sorry and make sure she was okay. That was it.

Ben sat in the car for hours, fiddling with his phone, trying to kill time until The Den closed. There were surprisingly a lot of cars there. Of course, very few bars outside Blackstone accepted shifters. He probably knew most of the people in there right now; many of them were his employees, looking to relax after a long, hard day working in the mines.

The lot began to empty, and he knew she would leave any moment. Sure enough, the Toyota came out and headed east. Ben turned the key in the ignition and went in the same direction. He spotted the car as it was entering the highway.

It was easy enough to follow the car; he could use his

enhanced sight to stay a respectable distance. If she noticed she was being followed, she didn't show it. The car continued down the freeway for a couple of miles without taking any exits. "Where the heck is she going?" Ben had thought maybe she lived in Blackstone or one of the neighboring towns, but they were driving much farther away.

He had been so distracted trying to figure out where she lived, he didn't notice that her car had slowed down, eased onto the shoulder, then completely stopped. He slammed on the brakes, then put the gear in reverse, pulling back until he was just in front of the Toyota. He glanced up in the rearview mirror.

The front door opened, and he heard a frustrated sigh, followed by a soft thunk, then a pained cry. He quickly exited the car and trudged toward her.

"Are you—"

Ben felt like someone had punched him in the gut. Air escaped his lungs as he drank in the sight of her. If he thought she was gorgeous from behind ... she was even more spectacular from the front. Wide, curvy hips dipped into a small waist. Tits that would certainly be more than a handful. Her skin was like marble, but he bet it would feel velvety smooth. Red coppery curls framed a beautiful, softly rounded face. As soon as their gazes clashed, he was knocked back into reality.

"... okay?"

Eyes the color of dark jade looked up at him curiously. He shut down the growl that was building inside him. The bear was scratching at him, grumbling and grunting something incoherent. *Shut up! Don't frighten her,* he begged.

She looked down at her feet. "Uhm ... my car broke down," she said in a soft voice.

"Oh. Right." Why did his throat suddenly feel dry?

She shuffled her feet.

"Do you have anyone you can call?" he asked, finally getting his head on straight. "Triple-A? A towing company? A neighbor?"

"I'm not really sure. I can't afford either of the first two, so I guess I could wake up my neighbor." She bit her lip, her white teeth digging into the soft, pink flesh in a way that made him stifle a groan.

"I can take you home."

Her head snapped up, and her eyes grew wide.

"I mean," he cleared his throat, "take you to *your* home." He wiped his hand on his pants and held it out to her. "I'm Ben. Ben Walker."

"I know who you are," she said. "I-I-I mean …."

There was a fear in her eyes that made him uncomfortable, and he instantly knew she recognized him. He dropped his hand. "I'm sorry. About the other night. You weren't hurt, were you?"

She shook her head. "I wasn't." Her eyes went wide. "Do you live near—wait, are you following me?" Her voice pitched higher, and he could hear the alarm in her tone. She staggered back until she hit the hood of her car.

Fuck. This wasn't what he wanted. But he supposed it was his fault, following a girl home in the dark of night like some creeper. "Don't be scared, please. I won't hurt you."

"Y-y-you turned … and now …."

"Yeah. I didn't mean to lose control like that. And I wasn't following you. I mean, I was …," he said in a sheepish tone as he scratched the back of his neck. "I just wanted to say I'm sorry and to check if you were okay … uh …."

"Penny," she offered. "Penny Bennet."

Penny. Pretty Penny. It suited her. "Penny. Why don't you let me take you home? As an apology. I promise, I'm not here to hurt you. You can take your phone out and have 911 on standby while we're in the truck."

She sucked in a deep breath, then exhaled. "I suppose. I mean, the people at the bar ... Heather and the other servers, they know you. I mean, they didn't say you were a creep or anything. So I suppose it's okay if you give me a ride home."

Ben didn't know if he felt reassured or alarmed by the fact that she would easily take a ride from a stranger. Of course, it was the middle of the night and there were no other cars on the highway. One thing was for sure, he was glad he followed her tonight. She could have been alone. Or worse.

He tamped down the snarl in his throat. "Where do you live?"

"Over in Greenville," she said. "I'll give you directions if you need them."

"Sure." He led her to the truck and opened the passenger side door for her. Penny gave him a grateful nod, then climbed inside. She was a little short, so it took her two tries to get in, which he thought was adorable, just like her shapely ass.

"So," he said as he turned the key in the ignition, "which way?"

She put her seatbelt on. "Just keep driving. It's the next exit."

He steered the car back onto the highway. As he drove, he tried to glance at her from the corner of his eye. Penny had squeezed herself all the way to the other side, and her hands were on her lap, fiddling with her purse. She was obviously nervous. It was practically mixed in with her scent, that slight bitter tinge of apprehension. He wished he could reassure her, but he would just have to show her he could be trusted.

The highway signs said the exit to Greenville was up next, so he prepared to turn.

"Just turn right after the exit ramp," she said. "It's not much farther."

He did as she instructed, turning onto the old country road.

"Over there," she said, pointing to the right. A sign propped up by the side of the road read 'East Community Housing.' There was a paved driveway that led to a row of trailers. "It's the last one on the left."

Ben pulled the truck in front of the trailer. It was a single wide, and while it wasn't big, it was neat, with cream siding and a blue roof. A white fence ran around the small front yard, which was still bare thanks to the melting snow. There was an evergreen tree to the side which probably provided some privacy and shade in the mornings.

"What? You've never been in a trailer park?" she asked.

He didn't realize he'd been staring. "We got trailers up in the mining site. For office and storage and stuff."

"Right." She let out a breath. "Well, thanks," she said as she reached for the door.

"No."

She froze.

Ben cleared his throat. "I mean, you should let me help you." He got out, walked over to her side, and opened the door. "It's still slippery from the snow." He held out his hand.

She ignored his hand as she slid down from the passenger seat on her own.

He tried not to let her reluctance to touch his hand bother him. "Let me walk you up."

"That's not necessary," she said quickly. "I mean, you've done a lot already."

"It's fine." He tried to grab her elbow, but she moved away.

"What do you want?" she asked, looking up at him. Her cheeks were pink from the cold, her breath coming out in short gasps as puffs of air escaped her lips.

"Huh?" He scratched his head. "I just want to help."

"But why?"

Why indeed. "I just ... I thought maybe you were hurt that night. I wanted to make sure you were okay."

"I'm fine," she huffed. "It's getting late. You should go." She turned around and began to walk to the front of her trailer.

His bear roared at him, and he wrestled down an urge building inside him. "Wait, Penny."

She stopped but didn't look at him. "What?"

"Will you be at work tomorrow?"

"Yes."

"Can I come see you? Before or after?"

Her shoulders sagged. "I think you should go home, Ben."

"I—"

"Please." She turned around to face him. Her skin was flushed. "Please leave me alone."

"I can't." That came out of nowhere, but he knew it was true. He was drawn to her. "Penny—"

"What do you mean you can't? You didn't even notice me that night, so what's different now?"

Huh? "Excuse me?" He came closer to her. "What are you talking about?"

"Th-that night of the engagement party," she stammered. "You bumped into me, put me aside, and then ignored me."

"I did?" He searched through his brain, trying to find the memory. "I just don't remember. I've only ever seen you last Saturday." But then he realized it wasn't the first time he had been around her. The scent. The first time he smelled it was a few weeks ago, at Catherine and Matthew's party. "I'm sorry. I was preoccupied." It came back to him. He had been excited for the engagement and to see his sister Amelia. She lived a couple of towns over and was hardly ever home. He remembered bumping into someone and then pushing her aside.

She sighed. "Anyway, it doesn't matter."

It obviously bothered her, which bothered him. "Look, Penny—"

"Goodnight, Ben," she said, turning away from him.

He watched her run to her house, jogging up the small porch quickly. He seemed rooted to the spot, unable to move until she was gone and the door closed behind her.

It was then he realized what his bear was trying to vocalize.

Mine.

CHAPTER 4

BEN STOOD in front of the door for what seemed like an eternity. Penny was his. His *mate*. The revelation hit Ben like a sack full of bricks to the gut.

That was what *mine* meant, right? His bear recognized her. It didn't know how to tell him. Well, it did, in its own fucked up way, tearing out of him and mauling the guy who hurt her.

Ben walked back to his truck, trying to put a coherent thought together. He wished his dad were here. He remembered James telling him about meeting Laura, his mate, for the first time. "I knew right away," he had said. "Well, my bear did. But I had to take it slow. She's human, so she didn't know these things. I wanted her right away, but I had to play by her rules."

Of course, Ben's arrival into their lives nearly derailed their relationship. His birth mom had died when he was only three years old and left him with James. His father hadn't even known he existed until that point, but was willing to take on the responsibility of a son. And much to her credit, Laura stepped up right away, despite having only been with James for a few months. "I fell in love with you the moment I saw you," Laura would tell him while he was growing up. "Maybe even sooner than I did with your dad," she'd joke with a knowing smile at James.

As Ben started up the truck, he wondered what he was supposed to do now. His instinct was to take care of her right away. He wanted nothing more than to make sure she never had to worry about anything else in her life. She wouldn't have to work at The Den and have those other men looking at her or trying to touch her. The mere thought of any other man around her was getting his bear agitated. Yeah, the sooner that happened the better. Then she could just stay home and take care of their cubs. Maybe four or five would be nice ....

But, thinking back to what his father had said, he had to respect that Penny was a human. He had to take it slow. Woo her. Be gentle. He knew where he could start. That piece of junk car of hers. He could tow it back to town, have J.D., their trusted mechanic, take a look and get it fixed for her. He'd rather get her a new car, but that could wait until later.

He'd go slow with her. *Yeah, that's it.* Penny was sweet and shy, and she probably would be confused at first. But, she was his mate, one that his bear recognized, and so that should be all that mattered. He would do whatever it took to win her.

Since it was late, Ben hitched Penny's car onto his truck, towed it all the way back to his cabin, and then woke up early the next day to take it to J.D.'s Garage in town. Soon, the car was ready and J.D. even offered one of the guys to help return it to Greenville. He and the other guy drove up with Ben leading the way. It was early yet, so they quietly parked the car in her driveway and left in his Jeep.

And now, two hours later, he was back at work in the mines. He had done his usual rounds inside, checking things over, and headed back to his trailer office to get paperwork done.

"Boss."

"Yeah?" He looked up. The door was halfway open and Boone, one of the workers, popped his head in. "What is it?"

"Security asked me to come check in with you."

"What for?"

"There're a couple guys outside, looking for you. I mean, they said they're looking for work."

"Shifters?"

"Yeah. Bears."

Ben put down the invoices he was examining. Walk-ins weren't unusual, especially since everyone knew the mine was always looking for shifters willing to put in the work. "All right, give me five and have security escort them over."

Boone nodded, then disappeared. A couple of minutes later, the door to his office opened. "Thanks, John," he said to their new head of security as he led the two men behind him in.

"Have a seat," Ben instructed. He watched as the two men looked at each other, shrugged, and then sat down on the chairs in front of his desk. As they came closer, his bear began to stir. *Hmm* .... That happened sometimes, when he was around new shifters, so he ignored it. "You guys looking for jobs?"

The one sitting on the right spoke up. "Yeah. We heard you folks hire people like us." He was the older of the two, with long, stringy blond hair and a scraggly beard. Definitely a bear shifter; he could sense the man's bear and see the glint in his eye. "Name's Tyler."

The younger man looked similar to Tyler, except his hair was cropped close to his head. "Are you father and son?" Ben asked.

"Nah, cousins," Tyler answered. "But Rick and I used to drive a rig together."

"Ah, so you guys are truckers?"

"Yeah. But business was slow; we had to be let go."

"Are you looking for seasonal work?"

"Huh?" Tyler looked confused.

"Uh, seasonal. I mean, just until the summer when things pick up for you?"

Tyler laughed. "No need for fancy words with us," he said. "We're just simple folk, right?"

Ben shifted in his seat. "Sure, yeah."

"We'd like to stay on, as long as it takes." The smile Tyler gave him was unnerving.

Ben wasn't sure why, but his bear seemed on edge. Not angry or out of control, but there was something about these people that didn't sit right with his animal. They smelled strange, too. He could detect the fur, but not their natural scent. It was like they were wearing cologne to mask their normal shifter smell. He took a calming breath.

"Does he speak?" Ben nodded to Rick.

"He does, but not too much. Right, boy?"

"Y-y-yes," Rick stammered.

"He's simple, see? His momma dropped him on his head when he was young." Tyler cackled. "But he's strong. And so am I. Don't let the age fool ya."

"Right." Two more guys could help their operations, plus Lennox Corp. was all about helping shifters and giving them jobs when no one else would. But there was something about them that just didn't feel right. He reached for some papers under his desk. "Well, Tyler, Rick. Why don't you guys fill out these forms," he handed the papers to them, "and then drop them off with security? I'll make sure HR gets them."

"Thank you, Boss," Tyler said with a wink.

Ben waited for them to leave, but the two men remain planted in their seats. "Was there anything else?"

Tyler looked at the application form. "Oh, no siree." He grabbed Rick by the elbow and pulled up the younger man. "We'll be on our way then, Mr. Walker, *sir*." The two men got up and left the office.

Ben had never gotten the heebie jeebies, but having those men in his office was probably the closest he had come to being creeped out. They had a strange vibe, and he just couldn't put his finger on what it was. And his bear? It was still pacing around uncomfortably.

"Yo, Ben!" The door opened again, knocking him out of his thoughts.

"Hey Nathan, what's up?"

Nathan walked over and plopped down in one of the chairs. "Who the hell were those guys?"

"They were looking for work."

Nathan gave an exaggerated shiver. "Was it me or did they have a creepy vibe?"

So it wasn't just me. "Yeah, huh?" He'd call HR in the morning and tell them to give the usual thanks-but-no-thanks reply. He put all thoughts of the duo aside and turned back to Nathan. "So, did you need anything?"

"Yeah, you got time?"

"Sure."

"Jason called. Said he wants to meet with you, me, and Luke at Lennox HQ. Matthew will be there, too."

"Did he say what it was about?"

Nathan shook his head. "Not over the phone, he said."

Ben stood up and grabbed his keys, wallet, and phone. "Must be important. Let's go."

CHAPTER 5

Penny rolled over to her back and sighed. The sun peeking in from behind the blinds was unusually bright, and she slapped a hand over her eyes to keep the light out.

After tossing and turning for hours, her body had told her brain, *"Enough!"* and forced it to shut down. Thank God, because she wouldn't be able to get through the day without her sleep. Turning to the small clock beside her bed, she realized it was nearly noon.

She still couldn't believe what had happened last night. Her stupid Toyota finally conked out and in the middle of the highway, too. She had been so frustrated and annoyed that she hadn't notice the large pickup truck backing up in front of her. And then he came out. She thought she was hallucinating, but no. It was definitely Ben Walker.

God, he was more handsome up close. Blue eyes like the sky on a clear day. Dark blond hair that was a tad overgrown and an even darker, thicker beard that only made him more attractive. She couldn't help but stare at him. And then he offered to give her a ride. She didn't even really protest. *Oh yes, Ben, take me home!*

She threw a pillow over her face. He could have been a psycho, and she jumped right into his truck. But there was just something about him that made her feel safe, and she wasn't sure why.

"You don't even know him," she said to no one in particular. Anyway, it was just a ride, right? What else was she supposed to do, being stuck in the middle of nowhere? So she accepted his offer, forgetting where she lived.

Penny groaned and rolled onto her stomach, burying her face in her pillow. It's not that she was ashamed of living in a trailer park, but Ben had never even been in one, which only made the gap between them that much more obvious. He probably grew up in some mansion while she'd never lived in anything bigger than this trailer.

You think you're better than me, Penny? Better than all of us?

Her mother's words rang in her brain.

Think you're so high and mighty, doncha?

Sweat broke out on her forehead.

Don't you know men only want one thing?

She was fourteen when it started.

Deep down inside, she knew her mother loved her. She'd tell herself that over and over again. Momma made sure they had a roof over their head ... using whatever means necessary. That usually meant a string of men who would move in and help out with the rent and bills, only to leave a few months later. Sometimes they would just sneak out in the middle of the night, other times, there would be loud fights that ended up with a lot of screaming, broken furniture, and tears.

Of course, when momma wasn't shacking up with her latest boyfriend, she'd be hitting up the bars, cozying up to any man who would buy her a drink. 'Cozying up' might be too soft of a word. Eleanor Bennet was the proverbial town bicycle—everyone got a ride. And it made Penny's life a living hell.

She didn't understand it at first. But as she grew up, the whispers became louder and clearer. The women at the supermarket who would give them the side-eye. The other parents who would stop talking when Eleanor walked into homeroom during parent-teacher conferences, dressed in sky-high heels and a short dress. Or even the teachers at her school, who would shake their heads when she would complain about her classmates teasing her.

It didn't help that puberty arrived early, and her curves came in the summer she turned thirteen. The normal teasing would have been bad enough, but with her mother's reputation, it had been worse. And she couldn't even count on Momma for comfort. No, as she blossomed into a woman, Eleanor had lashed back at her, accusing her of all kinds of things. She was a slut if she came home late or wore short shorts; hoity-toity if she stayed at home and didn't come out of her room for dinner with her and her latest boy toy. It seemed nothing she ever did could please Eleanor. And then it happened ….

She just wished … if her father had been more of a fit parent, if he wasn't drunk half of the time, then ….

Penny shook her head and sat up. She should be thankful for where she was now. She had a job, a place to live, and food to eat, paid for by her own hard work.

But, still, it only cemented the thought that she and Ben were like oil and water. They would never mix together. What would his family think if he got involved with someone like her?

I can't.

His words puzzled her and made her feel things she shouldn't feel, for the reasons she just told herself. Okay, so maybe he was attracted to her physically. She knew men liked to look at her. But it would never work out between them.

Determined to put all thoughts of Ben aside, Penny swung her legs over the side of the bed, walked to the small bathroom, and got ready for the day. She was thankful The Den was able to open so soon. She had considered getting a second job but loved having afternoons to herself before her shift. She winced, thinking that she didn't have a choice now; the car repairs would surely put her into an even deeper hole. How would she even get to work today?

"No use crying over spilt milk," she said aloud as she poured some juice into a mug. She took a sip and strode to the front door. As she looked out the window, she nearly dropped the mug. Her car was sitting in the driveway.

Grabbing her coat and slipping into her discarded boots, Penny raced down the steps all the way to the car. It was definitely her car—her keys with The Little Mermaid key chain were sitting on the hood. But who …?

Who else? Ben. How …? Did he tow it all the way back here with his truck?

She touched the hood. It was still warm. That meant it had been running. She grabbed the keys, opened the door, slipped in, and turned on the ignition. The engine roared to life and purred.

"No, no, no, no!" She laid her head on the steering wheel. This couldn't be. Why the heck would he do this after she told him to stay away?

She didn't want to owe him. She sighed and lifted her

head. "I'll pay him back," she said in a determined voice. "Every cent."

As she drove into Blackstone, Penny realized she didn't even know where to find him. Did he have an office in town? Heather mentioned he was head of some mining operation, but she didn't know the first place to start looking. A quick internet search on Ben Walker and Blackstone turned up very little except the Lennox Corporation's corporate website, all generic and nothing about the location of any mines.

As she drove down Main Street, an idea popped in her head. Maybe Ben had an office at Lennox Corporation. *They must have their headquarters in Blackstone somewhere.* She stopped the car and punched in 'Lennox Corporation' on her GPS app.

"Bingo!" It wasn't far from where she was right now. After pressing 'Go Now,' she followed the device's instructions. She still wasn't very familiar with Blackstone, having never really gone anywhere except Main Street and The Den. It wasn't a sprawling city by any means, but Blackstone was one of the largest towns in the area, so it was still tricky to navigate for newcomers like her.

She turned right from the main road and saw the signs with Lennox Corporation's red and black logo. Slowing the car down, she stopped right across the street from the large office building, which was just outside the main part of town.

"Now what?"

Penny supposed she could walk in and ask where Ben's office was. The thought made her cringe, and she looked down at her worn jeans and sweater. It wasn't exactly office appropriate. If she went in, the receptionist would probably look down her nose at her. Plus, what would she do if she did see him? She didn't have any money now to give him. *This was a mistake. I should leave.* But how else was she going to pay him back?

A tapping on the window made her start. A familiar face looking at her from the outside made her sigh in relief, and she rolled her window down.

"Penny! It is you," Christina Stavros said in an excited voice, her light blue eyes sparkling.

"Christina! What are you doing here?"

She jerked her thumb at the building. "Sybil just dropped me off. I'm here to see Jason. What are you doing outside Lennox?"

Penny froze. She considered lying to the other woman, but what was she supposed to say? That she got lost? "Uhm, I'm looking for someone."

"Who are you looking for?"

She mumbled under her breath.

"I beg your pardon?"

"Ben." She cleared her throat. "Walker. Ben Walker."

Christina frowned. "Why? I ... Oh! I heard about what happened the other night." Christina leaned down and placed her arms on the window. "Are you hurt? Do you need to pay for medical bills or something? Because you know Matthew will take care of that."

Penny shook her head. "Oh no. Not at all. Er ...," she took a deep breath, "I just need to talk to him."

"Well, as far as I know, Ben doesn't have an office here." Christina tapped a finger on her chin. "But we could ask Jason or Matthew. C'mon."

"What?" Before she could protest, Christina unlocked her

door, opened it, and tugged her out. "No! I mean, really, it's fine. I can find him another time."

But it was no use. Christina dragged her out of her car and across the street toward the imposing building. She tried not to look at the security guards who gave them curious stares, though no one stopped them, not even the stern-looking receptionist who waved them in.

"I'm actually glad I found you," Christina said as they entered the elevator. She punched the number at the top and the door closed.

"Really? Why?"

"We need to start your self-defense lessons."

Penny laughed nervously. "Oh, I didn't think you were serious about that."

The elevator stopped and Christina led her out. They walked to the end of the hall where there were two doors and two empty desks. "Matthew and Jason don't have assistants yet," she explained as they entered the door on the left. "We can talk and wait in here."

They walked into the plush office, and Christina motioned for her to sit down on the couch. "Coffee or tea?" she asked.

"I'm fine. Maybe some water if you have it?"

"Sure." Christina strode over to the small refrigerator in the corner and grabbed two bottles of water. She gave one to Penny and sat down next to her. "Now, about those lessons."

"You don't really have to do that," Penny said. "I know you were just being nice."

"Penny." Christina put a hand over hers. "I meant what I said about learning how to defend yourself."

A lump began to form in her throat. "Why are you being so nice to me?" Penny asked.

"Why shouldn't I be?" Christina said.

"I told you, I'm nobody," Penny reminded her. "I'm just a waitress. No one important."

Christina's nostrils flared. "You have every right to defend yourself against anyone who wants to hurt you. You shouldn't have to be afraid, especially if someone hurt you in the past."

Penny felt the blood drain from her face and her chest tightened, like a giant fist wrapped around her torso and squeezed.

Memories flooded back in her mind. No matter how hard she tried, she couldn't push them back, not anymore.

The room suddenly felt small, and she was back. Back to where it began. Where it ended. That tiny bathroom in her mother's trailer. Sitting on the toilet, pushing her hands against the door to keep it closed. Not that it would help. He was much bigger. Much stronger. He would break that door at any moment. She could feel the vibrations on the wood as he pounded with his meaty fists. She remembered the hot tears flowing down her cheeks. But now they weren't just memories because she could feel the wetness gathering in her eyes.

"Penny. Penny!"

"N-n-no...stop!" But her cries fell on deaf ears. It only egged him on and the door shook violently. "Please!"

Hands grabbed her arms and shook her. "Penny, snap out of it!"

And she remembered where she was. Christina's light blue eyes were wide as saucers, her mouth open.

"I ... I'm sorry." She stood up and gathered her purse. The heat on her cheeks was so intense, it felt like someone had tossed kerosene on them and lit a match. "I should go."

Christina grabbed her arm and whipped her around.

"Penny, please stay and talk to me. Or you can talk to a professional."

Penny covered her face with her palms. "No, I'm fine. I swear, I just ... I haven't slept well."

"If someone hurt you—"

"No!" she shrieked, but quickly shut her mouth. "Please, I have to go."

Before Christina could protest further, Penny pivoted and scurried away. She yanked the door open and took a step forward but collided into a very large, solid object. No, it wasn't an object. As if her humiliation wasn't bad enough, she ran right into Ben Walker.

"Penny? What are you—hey, are you okay?" His large hands gripped her arms as she stopped. Taking a deep breath, she inhaled his aftershave. That and the warmth emanating from his body sent a calming feeling over her, and she closed her eyes. "Penny?"

Her eyes flew open.

"What's wrong? Are you crying?"

"I—" She looked back and saw Christina staring at her. She knew that look. It was pity. Her head whipped back to Ben. "I'm fine," she snapped and disentangled herself from him, then walked away.

"Penny, wait!"

She ignored him and picked up her pace. Not that it helped, with his longer strides, he quickly caught up and stepped in front of her. "Penny, what's the matter? Is the car okay? Because I can have J.D. take a look at it again."

Right. The car. "It's fine. I mean ... you shouldn't have done that!"

He frowned. "Shouldn't have? What was I supposed to do? Let you walk all the way to work?"

She put her hands up in exasperation. "I mean, you shouldn't have done anything! I told you to leave me alone!"

"I did leave last night."

"I meant, leave me alone *forever!*" She side stepped past him and strode away angrily, hoping he would get the message.

Poor Penny. Poor Penny with her good-for-nothing drunk dad and her floozy mom. This was why she hated Colorado and was glad she left to live with Grams in Texas where no one knew her. In Houston no one threw a pity party for poor Penny. No one knew what happened that night when the cops came to their trailer and broke down the door. Or the humiliation she suffered afterward and the hate, not just from neighbors and friends, but her own mother.

She took the elevator down to the lobby and ran out after pushing on the heavy glass doors with all her might. The cool air felt good as it entered her lungs, and she let out a long breath before she dashed to her car.

CHAPTER 6

Ben stared after Penny as she disappeared into the elevator, feeling dumbfounded. What just happened? And what was she doing at Lennox?

"Ben?" Christina, Jason's fiancée, touched his arm. "Everything okay?"

"Huh?" He looked down at her. "What was she doing here?"

"Penny? I'm sorry, I didn't know." Christina's face fell.

"Know? Know what?" He grabbed her shoulders.

"I mean, I can't be sure."

Ben shook her. "Sure of what? What did she want?"

"She wanted to see you," Christina said in a shaky voice. "She didn't tell me what for."

"Get your hands off her."

The hallway suddenly went cold and a prickly sensation crawled over his skin. His bear let out an angry growl, rearing up and getting ready for a fight.

"I'm warning you, Ben." Jason's voice was deadly serious, the barely contained fury evident. "Let. Her. Go."

Ben dropped his hands to his sides and turned around to face his cousin. Much to his surprise, Christina stepped in between them.

"It's fine, it's all fine," she said in a soothing voice. She placed a hand on Jason's chest. "Ben didn't hurt me."

"Why was he shaking you?" Jason's eyes glowed, and Ben could feel the dragon inside him, ready to rip out at any moment. Behind him, Luke and Nate were silent, but the tension in their bodies was unmistakable.

"He was just worried," Christina said. She slipped her arms around Jason's waist.

"I'm sorry," Ben said. "I didn't mean to." He shook his head, trying to wrap his head around why Penny would be here, of all places.

"What the hell happened?" Jason asked.

"It's okay," Christina said. "Let's go inside your office and talk, okay?"

The guys followed Christina into Jason's office, closing the door behind him.

"Talk," Jason said, crossing his arms over his chest.

"Penny was looking for Ben," Christina explained, then looked at Ben. "I saw her outside and told her she could come in and we could ask Matthew where to find you."

"I thought that was her running out of the lobby, but I wasn't sure," Nathan said. "She looked scared."

"She had some kind of anxiety attack. It was before you came in," Christina assured Ben.

"Why?" Ben asked. "What did you do?" Jason sent him a warning glare. He cleared his throat. "I mean, what were you two doing here?"

"We were just talking about that night at The Den."

"What night?" Ben asked, his stomach twisting.

Christina looked at Jason warily, but continued when he nodded. "Penny was attacked."

"What?"

"Ben, calm down," Nathan said. "It's fine. She's fine. Nothing happened. Christina saved her."

Claws ripped at him. He should have been there. It shouldn't have happened at all. "Where is he? Is he in jail? I'm going to—"

"It doesn't matter," Jason said.

Ben wanted to throttle his cousin but stifled the urge. He would find out more about this man who tried to hurt Penny. "So, she's still traumatized by what happened?"

"Yes, but I don't think it was just that." Christina's tone became serious. "You know, I've seen many people who've gone through trauma in my job. I think it was more than just that one time. I think … she might have been hurt in the past."

Ben scrubbed his palms down his face. Penny's words … her face … she might not have known what he *really* was, but she could probably feel it. If she had faced evil before, she knew what it looked like. *Leave me alone forever.* He was a monster. He was born a monster and would always be one.

"I have to go." He walked toward the door, but as he tried to get away, a hand wrapping around his forearm jerked him back.

An inhuman growl escaped his throat, and his bear was getting too near the surface. "Let go, Luke," he said in the calmest voice he could muster.

Luke's tawny eyes were ablaze. The lion inside him was not afraid. "You've been like this for months. No one has noticed, but *I* do."

Luke's lion was just as fucked up as his bear, so it didn't

surprise him that he noticed. "It's nothing." He tugged his arm away. "And if you touch me again, I swear to God—"

"Ben, what the fuck is wrong with you?" Jason asked. "This isn't you."

Of course they didn't think so. They always saw him as Ben Walker, the responsible one. Even growing up, he was the one breaking up the fights and stopping everyone from getting into trouble. "I gotta go." He ignored their calls and headed toward the stairs. He couldn't take the elevator; he knew he'd smell her there. *Penny.* Sweet and beautiful Penny. She was right to run away and reject him. Because no beast like him should have a mate.

Ben barely made it back to his cabin before his bear ripped out of his skin. He wasn't sure where it took him—miles away probably because when he woke up hours later, he was exhausted. *At the least the damn thing didn't make me walk back.* He woke up on his porch, naked, and his body covered in healing scratches.

He was breaking apart from the inside. Penny's reaction to him and what happened to her in the past ... it all made sense. He couldn't stop thinking about it. Penny being hurt. He wished he could change the past, so it never happened to her. His bear was raging, wanting to kill whoever had done that to her. To his mate.

He went inside his cabin and headed straight for the shower. The water felt good on his skin, especially when it washed away the dirt and blood. As he was getting dressed afterward, he heard the front doorbell ring.

Ben considered ignoring it, but the persistent sound

wouldn't stop. With an annoyed grunt, he walked down from his bedroom to the front door and yanked it open.

"What do you want?"

He was caught by surprise at who it was. He expected Matthew. Maybe even Jason or Nathan. Not Luke.

"Are you gonna let me in or are you just gonna stare?"

Dumbfounded, he stepped aside and let the other man in. "What are you doing here?"

"What? I can't check on ya?"

Ben crossed his arms over his chest. Luke had been barely showing up to any family events in the last couple of years. He didn't come to dinners at the castle or go out during graduations, anniversaries, and other celebrations. In fact, he only showed up during public events, like Aunt Riva's retirement and Matthew's wedding. He suspected it was because he didn't want to humiliate his mother, which made Ben think Luke hadn't quite given up on his adoptive family.

Luke crossed the living room and went straight into his kitchen. A few seconds later, he came out with the six-pack that had been sitting in the fridge. He popped one can open and took a swig before placing the rest on the coffee table. "Now, what the fuck is going on with you."

"I don't know—"

"Don't give me that bullshit, Ben," Luke interrupted. "We both know you've been fighting your bear for months. You've also been trying to hide it from us. But I've seen your bear tear up more than just trees. I've seen it at night, roaming the mountains."

Goddamn Luke and his nightly patrols. "It's fine. I'm fine, just letting off steam."

Luke chugged the rest of the beer and threw the can aside. "I said don't bullshit me."

"Did you come in here to drink my beer and mess up my house?" Ben countered, his hands tightening into fists at his sides. "Because if so, there's the door, don't let it hit ya on the way out."

"Ben, what the fuck happened with your bear?"

"Nothing." There was nothing that happened because it had always been like that.

"And the girl? What's her name? Penny, right?"

Hearing her name unleashed his bear, and he could feel the muscles underneath his hands flex as his claws emerged. He took a deep breath. "What about her?"

"She yours? Your mate? Is that why you've been acting like this?"

"Stay out of this." He turned his back and looked down at his hands. Fur was sprouting on his palms, and he could feel his hands turning into paws.

Luke huffed. "Why the hell are you all such shits when it comes to women? First Matthew, then Jason, and now you."

Ben whipped his head around. "What are you talking about?"

"Ignoring her ain't gonna help your bear."

"What am I supposed to do? Didn't you hear what Christina said? She's been through enough; she doesn't need me fucking up her life even more!"

"You're a damn fool, Ben," Luke roared.

"I'm a monster! And you know it. You can feel it. You've seen it." Ben could feel his bear's canines growing and he closed his mouth to keep Luke from seeing them.

"You're no monster," Luke spat. "You want to show me what a big, bad bear you are?" He stretched his arms out. "I can take you."

"Stop!" Ben growled, his voice half human, half bear. "Don't make me—"

"Shit. You're no monster. I know what you are. You're going to be the good guy," Luke said. "You're going to leave her alone because you think she's too good for you."

"She *is* too good for me." Ben shrank back, the reality hitting him in the gut. Penny … she had been through enough, obviously. She didn't need to be stuck with him and his bad blood. He huffed to himself. He'd been a fool, thinking about a future and cubs with her. Any cubs they would have would just be fucked up like him. No, this would stop with him. This bad blood wasn't going to spread further.

"Get out."

"Ben—"

"I said get out of my house." He could barely control himself. If Luke didn't leave … he didn't know what he'd do. He didn't bother waiting for Luke to answer or leave. He turned away and walked up the stairs before slamming the door to his bedroom.

Exhaustion began to seep into his bones, and he fell on the bed and closed his eyes.

CHAPTER 7

Penny pulled into her parking spot at The Den and turned off the engine. She let out a sigh and then lay her head on the wheel. *Damn. Damn. Damn.* She really didn't want to be here. She wished she was back in Houston. Or anywhere really. Anywhere but Blackstone.

She barely survived last night. After what happened at Lennox Corp., she considered calling off her shift, but she couldn't. She had to pay back Ben. So she went right to work.

It had been a disaster. She kept mixing up orders and bumping into people. Then, she dropped a whole tray of glasses because her hands were still shaking. She hadn't had an episode like that in a long time. Once in a while, sure. Certainly after that customer cornered her when she was taking a break. She usually got over it. She was used to just pushing it out of her mind. But it happened in front of Christina and then she ran into Ben and just lost it.

Oh Ben. He was so sweet and kind. He didn't know what he'd be getting into with her, and it was best he didn't find out. The ugliness and the shame was too much. Her reputation followed her like a stink, and he would have found out, eventually.

The clock on her dash told her it was time to punch in. "Another day, another dollar," she muttered as she stepped out of her car and walked to the employee entrance in the back of the bar.

"Penny."

She stopped in her tracks and turned around. "Yes?" She squinted at him.

The man looked familiar. Where had she seen him before? He was tall, even by Blackstone shifter standards, probably as tall as Ben, though not as broad. His long blond hair was tied back in a messy bun and those eyes—they were like molten gold.

"Luke. Lennox."

Ah yes, she remembered. "Uhm, so is there anything you needed?"

"It's about Ben."

"Ben?" A strange feeling swept over her. "Is he okay? Is he hurt?"

"Something like that."

Coldness gripped her, and she stepped forward. "Is he in the hospital? Oh God, is he okay?" She told him she wanted him to leave her alone forever but not like this.

"He will be. If you come with me."

A group of girls—Olive, Mia, and one other server—walked past and then turned around and gave them strange looks. "I can't," she whispered. "I have to get to work."

"I cleared it with Tim," he said. "We can take my truck."

Penny hesitated for a moment, but her instinct was telling her to go to Ben. "All right. If you say it's fine."

She followed him across the lot to the black Chevy truck parked in the middle. He opened the door for her, and she climbed in.

"Where are we going?" she asked as they drove away from The Den. "The hospital?"

"No." Luke kept his gaze straight on the road.

This was probably the part where she should start screaming and try to get out, but something was telling her that Luke would never hurt her. He was Ben's friend, right? And a Lennox. He wouldn't try to kidnap her.

Luke was driving toward Main Street, so she knew that was at least a good sign. When he pulled up in front of Rosie's Bakery and Cafe, she gave him a strange look. "Luke? What's going on? What's wrong with Ben?"

He let out a sigh. "I'm doing this for both your sakes."

"What do you mean?"

He nodded to the window. Christina was sitting at one of the tables. "I know you don't trust me, but you trust her, right?"

"S-s-sure. But I don't understand what's going on."

"You should talk to her, so you can understand what's happening." He got out of his side, walked across the front, and opened the door for her. "I promise, it'll be fine." He held his hand out to her. "I'll bring you back to The Den any time you want, but hear her out. Please. It's for Ben."

Penny stared at his hand. She guessed he wasn't the type to ask favors from anyone, but something about the way he asked made her heart wrench. "Fine." She took his hand and allowed him to help her down. "If it's for—"

"What the fuck is going on?"

The surrounding air suddenly felt thick and cold. Penny whipped her head to the right. Ben was standing there, hands fisted at his side, his body tense. Anger didn't even begin to describe the look on his face. She tried to open her mouth to speak, but nothing came out.

Ben turned to Luke. "So, is this why you came to me last night?"

"What?"

"You came to my house, pretending to care about me, but really," his eyes narrowed at their hands, "you wanted her for yourself."

Luke dropped her hand. "What are you talking about?"

Ben lunged forward and grabbed Luke by the front of his shirt. "You know *who* she is. Were you trying to see if I was going to back off before you tried to take her away from me?"

What was going on? "Ben, please—"

Luke pushed at Ben with all his might, making him stagger back. "Don't touch me ever again."

"Or what?" Ben roared, stretching to his full height. "You've already done the worst thing you could do to me!"

Ben's eyes began to glow and the muscles under his skin were crawling and stretching. *Oh no.* She knew what that meant.

"She's *mine!*" he growled.

"Stop!" Penny threw herself toward Ben, placing her trembling hands on his chest. "Ben, please, don't." She didn't want a repeat of the other night. She knew he had gotten in big trouble; Tim had told the staff Ben Walker was not welcome at The Den for the time being.

Ben let out a harsh grunt and stepped back. "So, you want me to leave you alone, huh? But you go out with him?"

Penny gasped. "What are you talking about?"

"You … and Luke," he spat.

"You think he and I … that we're …" She put her hands up

in frustration. "I came here for you! Because I thought you were hurt."

"Hurt?" he asked.

"Yeah, that's what Luke said! And then it turns out it was just a ruse." Her brows knitted into a frown. "Is this some sick game you're playing? For kicks? Trying to see the poor girl from the trailer park break? Because I've had about enough!" She threw up her hand in frustration and walked away. If she saw Ben Walker again, it would be too soon.

Penny wasn't sure where she was going. She was stuck out here with no way to get back to The Den where she'd parked her car. There was no one she could call for a ride and no money for a cab even if she could find one. She had to somehow find her way back to The Den. Squaring her shoulders, she decided this was better than being back there with Ben and Luke. *Stupid men.*

Twenty minutes later, she was walking down a dark, deserted road. When she had driven this way, it seemed quicker. And brighter. And less scary. She shivered and rubbed her hands together but was determined to keep moving.

Stupid, stupid Penny. Falling for Luke's lie. And Christina? Was she part of this? She had thought the other woman was nice. Maybe she was just like those rich, snobby girls in high school. The ones who would laugh at her thrift store clothes and walk over to her table during lunch to check if her bag was a knockoff. She had learned to ignore those girls, but their cruelty stung.

And Ben? What was his part in all this?

The hum of an engine came closer from behind and the beams from headlights were getting bigger. Penny moved farther away from the edge of the road, hoping whoever it was didn't see her.

The vehicle began to slow down until it was right beside her, then the windows rolled down.

"Penny. Penny!"

She picked up her pace when she heard Ben's voice, which was a silly thing, she knew. He was in a car; she could never outrun him. Still, she kept going.

"Penny, c'mon," Ben called out as he continued to follow her.

The sound of tires screeching on gravel and the click of a door unlocking didn't slow her down, nor did the footsteps that were getting closer and closer. However, when she heard the one word from his mouth, she stopped in her tracks.

"Please."

Her heart jerked forward like one of those crash test dummies when the car hits the wall. That word and the sincerity in his voice shook her to her very core. Slowly, she turned to face him.

Ben was breathing hard, his shoulders were slumped over, and his eyes glowed in the dim light. "Penny. I'm sorry. For what I said back there about you and Luke."

"You thought I was on a date with him?"

"He told me what was going on. And then Christina came out and explained. That they had set this whole thing up."

"They set this up? I don't understand."

He sighed. "Look, can we talk? Please?"

She wanted to say no. She should say no and tell him and his crazy bunch of friends to leave her alone. But the look on his face was making her heart wrench. Desperation. Anguish.

And she wanted to be the one to make it all go away. "Fine. Explain."

He rubbed his palms over his beard. "Luke, Jason, and Christina thought they were helping. I was trying to do what you asked—leave you alone—but they just couldn't let it go."

"Let what go?"

"They were just meddling, you see? She was going to talk to you and tell you—" He stopped short and gritted his teeth.

"Tell me what?" she asked. "What, Ben?"

He remained silent, his jaw going tense. "I shouldn't."

"Ben." She took a step closer to him, her heart racing in her chest. "Ben." She wanted to ask him the question that had been lingering in her mind since she walked away. The one about his words that had been branded into her brain. "Ben, what did you mean when you said I was yours?"

He hesitated for a moment and let out a pained grunt. "That you're mine. My mate."

The air rushed out of her lungs, and she suddenly felt dizzy. The words didn't make sense in her brain, but they made her shiver. "I don't understand. I'm not a shifter."

"I know," he said. "You don't have to be. I mean, it's probably confusing and I can't explain it either. It's just a feeling. My bear chose you."

She gasped. "You can't mean that."

He nodded. "It's true. It seems fast for you but—"

"No, no, no!" She shook her head. "You can't. I mean, you don't want me!"

"What?" He reached for her, but she evaded his grasp. "Of course I want you!"

"But you can't!" She turned around and wrapped her arms around herself. "You can't want someone like me."

"Like what?" he asked.

Pain gripped her like a fist, tightening and squeezing every last bit of life from her body until she couldn't breathe. "Believe me. You don't want me. I'm not the type of girl you want to introduce to y-your parents or your friends."

She felt him come closer, slowly, but he didn't make a move to touch her. "Is it because ... Christina told me you had an episode in Jason's office. She thinks something happened to you ... someone did something to you ... something terrible."

His words hung in the air for a moment before she spoke. "It *was* terrible."

"How ... terrible?"

Penny's bottom lip trembled. "He didn't get to touch me. But I was terrified and ...."

"So you weren't—"

She shook her head. She supposed it was a logical conclusion. "But he tried."

"Who?" Ben's voice was clipped.

"M-m-my momma's boyfriend. John." It had been years since she said that name or even anything about the incident aloud. After what happened, she'd actually tried to talk to a counselor and go to group therapy, but it was too much. For one thing, she felt ashamed because those women had suffered real trauma. But, then, what happened to her had been so awful, she didn't know what to do.

"I was sixteen. He was practically living with us. And ... and one night Momma was stuck at work, covering another shift. I came home late because I was s-s-studying for a test." Her vision swam in front of her, and she took a deep breath. "He accused me of having sex with some boy at school. We were just lab partners!" Her body was shaking now. She could never forget what he had said. The things he had accused her of doing. And what had happened next. "And then he ... he grabbed me. I got away and locked myself in the bathroom. I was crying, and he was screaming and trying to break down the door." Tears began to pour down her face. "Our neighbors must have heard because the cops came before he could get to me."

Ben let out a relieved sigh. "So nothing ... happened?"

"No. Not like that." John never got his hands on her. In fact, no man had ever touched her.

"I'm so glad ... I mean, I'm sorry. What you went through was still awful. But it wasn't your fault."

"I know." She wiped the tears with the back of her hand. That's what Marian, her social worker had said. Marian had been her support. The only one who believed her.

"Penny." He stepped closer and tried to touch her arm, but she shrank away. "I'm sorry. But that doesn't matter to me. What happened to you in the past? I wish to God it hadn't, but that doesn't mean you can't be my mate."

"T-t-that's not why."

"I don't understand."

"That's not the end of it." She took a deep breath, wondering if she should continue. He had to understand. "John was Greenville High's football coach. Led the team to two championships, about to go for a third. The cops, they arrived in time to stop him, but when I tried to press charges, t-t-they discouraged me. He was drunk, that's all. Couldn't control himself. They said it would bring a lot of trouble. But the social worker assigned to me, Marian, said I should press charges. So I did." She fidgeted with the bottom of her shirt. "But he said I was coming on to him. That I was the one trying to seduce him."

A low, guttural growl startled her. She realized it was from Ben. "Go on," he said in a tight voice.

"Then the football team started spreading lies about me. That I was ... that I had been with all of them." She could still hear all the names they called her. And see all the nasty things they had written on her locker.

"Surely someone believed you."

"My social worker did. But half the town didn't." And the other half? Well, it seemed all they cared about was the championship.

"And your mother?"

Penny winced. If she were truly honest with herself, that was what hurt most of all. How could a mother not believe her own daughter? It had taken her years to figure out why. Eleanor had been jealous. Jealous that her daughter was younger and that her own good looks were fading. Jealous that her own boyfriend's roving eyes had fixed on her Penny. She knew this was why Eleanor had sided with John, but couldn't say it out loud.

The curse Ben muttered under his breath told her she didn't have to. "What happened then? You got out of there? Where was your dad?"

"My daddy couldn't take care of me. He was an alcoholic and didn't have a job and there was no way social services was going to place me with him. So they found my Grams, his mom, living out in Houston." The day she left Greenville was the happiest day of her life.

"And your mother?"

She shrugged. "Last I heard, she and John got married and he's still coaching." She did her best to avoid going into town. She shopped, filled up her tank, even went to the mechanic miles out of her way just so she wouldn't run into anyone she knew. But it seemed she still couldn't avoid her past as evidenced by the other night when Kyle and his friends had come in to The Den.

Penny turned away, trying to hide the shame on her face. "So you see, you can't get mixed up with—"

He was suddenly in front of her. "No!"

How did he move so fast?

Ben put his hands on her shoulders gingerly. His skin was so warm, the contact barely there. "Penny, I told you, I don't care about that."

"It follows me around like a stink. Those guys who were bothering me at The Den that night? They were from my high school. They still remember. You don't know what that means now, but you will. And you'll regret it once those old stories are mucked up again."

He let out a deep sigh. "How can I convince you that I just want you?"

"Your *bear* wants me," she pointed out. "Don't you get a choice in this?"

"I *am* my bear. It's hard to explain. But trust me, I want to be with you so bad. The first time you bumped into me? I may not have seen you, but I knew who you were. You were there in the back of my mind this whole time. And seeing you again couldn't have been a coincidence. Penny, please. Give this a chance."

She wanted to say no. She should say no and save themselves the trouble.

But what if you say yes?

The voice in the back of her mind was clear. What if she did say yes?

"I'm not good at this. I've never had a relationship. I've never even been with anyone." Heat stole into her face. Did he understand what she just admitted to? She looked up at him, trying to assess his gaze. "But ... we can try."

Ben's shoulders relaxed. "We can take things slow. As slow as you want." His fingers touched her cheek, and she shivered. He pulled away. "I'm sorry. I won't touch you without asking."

"No." She grabbed his hand and held it up. "It's okay. That felt nice." She closed her eyes and placed his large palm on her cheek. It was warm and callused. A feeling of contentment settled over her. It was so different from when anyone else tried to touch her.

"Can I take you out to dinner?"

Her eyes flew open, and she let go of his hand. "Like a date?"

"Yes. Tomorrow, though, not now. You should probably go home now and get some rest. I can drive you back to your car."

"I probably won't be able to get another night off until next week."

"That's okay. We finish work at the mines early. I can pick you up and we can have dinner before your shift."

"Okay." The butterflies in her stomach were fluttering with nervousness and anticipation. A date with Ben? She couldn't believe this was happening.

"Let's get you back home then." Ben led her back to his Jeep, opened the door for her, and helped her inside.

Five minutes later, Ben pulled up behind her car in the parking lot of The Den. "Hold on," he said. He got out, walked over to her side, and opened the door for her.

"You don't have to keep doing that," she said wryly.

"I do. I mean, my mom would throw a fit if I didn't," he said with a chuckle.

The mention of his mother made her stomach flip flop and not in a good way, but she pushed that feeling aside for now. "Thank you," she said as she walked over to the driver's side door of her car. "Oh! The repairs! You have to let me pay you back."

He shook his head. "No way."

"Ben," she warned.

"Fine, you pay me back when you can," he said with a smile. It made his face look boyish, even with his thick beard. "I'll follow you home."

"It's out of your way," she protested. "I'll be okay."

"But I won't be, not until I know you're home safe."

She knew she wasn't going to win this argument. "All right."

She got into her car and pulled out of her spot. Just as he promised, Ben followed her for the whole drive back to her home, keeping enough distance between them so he didn't blind her with his headlights but not so much that he lost her.

Were they really going to do this? Dating? Was that even what it was called with shifters. *Oh my God. I'm going on a date with a guy who turns into a giant bear!* The thoughts reeling around in her head nearly made her pass out, but she kept her eyes on the road. Should she call things off now? Her brain was telling her yes, but that voice in her head kept saying no.

When she pulled into her driveway, an idea popped into her head. She had to be sure before this all went too far. Instead of heading in, she walked back to his Jeep and climbed up on the running board, then knocked on his window.

The glass rolled down. "Everything okay?" His brows were drawn together in concern.

"No. I mean, yes!" *Don't chicken out now.* "I need a favor."

"Anything you want."

"Kiss me."

For a brief moment, desire flashed in his eyes, but it was quickly replaced by confusion. "Excuse me?"

"Kiss me." She had to know. "Please."

His hand snaked out and his fingers threaded through her hair, then pulled her closer. She gasped as his lips came closer, but instead of mashing his mouth against hers as she expected, he brushed his lips softly against hers, his beard tickling her in a pleasant way. He was gentle, and slow, as he had promised. And so warm and soft. The touch sent her knees wobbling, and she had to hang on to the door to keep from toppling back.

"Was that okay?" he asked as he pulled away. His eyes were glazed over, his stare intense.

A small gasp of disappointment escaped her lips. "Yeah." More than okay. She had tried dating in the past, but each time her date would try to kiss her, she would freeze. The memories would come back and she would push the guy away. But with Ben, it was the complete opposite. She wanted him to kiss her more.

"Penny?" He was looking at her with confusion again.

"Oh, right." She gave him a shy smile. "I'll see you tomorrow?"

"I'll pick you up at four?"

She nodded. She was afraid she was going to do something embarrassing like squeak with excitement. Or grab his head and kiss him so she could feel his lips again. Letting go of the window, she hopped off his Jeep and scampered to the safety of her front door. When she closed it behind her and clicked the lock, she heard the vehicle drive away.

Penny leaned her head back against the door and let out a breath. She touched her lips; they felt branded, like she would never forget the feel of his mouth on hers. She shivered in anticipation. What would their date be like? And after?

"Oh God." She walked to the bathroom to get ready for bed. Hopefully, she'd be able to sleep tonight.

CHAPTER 8

Ben whistled to himself happily as he drove toward Greenville. As soon as he finished work, he had gone straight home to shower and get ready for his date. He'd been thinking about Penny the whole day, and now he was finally on the way to see her.

After she ran from him, he had vowed to stay away from her, for her own good. But seeing Penny and Luke together had driven him into a jealous rage. He felt foolish now, especially after Christina showed up and explained everything. Luke had told Jason and Christina what he suspected, and she was just trying to help Penny understand. She'd even arranged for Penny to have the night off so they could get dinner together, but then she had some emergency and couldn't pick her up, so she asked Luke to do it.

Ben felt about ten inches tall after all that. He had accused Penny of dating Luke behind his back. He knew he had to make it up to her, so he chased her down to apologize.

He thought for sure she'd run away when he revealed that his bear had chosen her for a mate. Instead, she opened herself up to him. He gripped the steering wheel tight, thinking back on what she had told him about her past. He'd thought the worst, of course, but hearing that her mom's asshole boyfriend didn't touch her made him feel relieved. Though, it didn't matter to him if something did happen to her; he wanted to be with her either way. However, he knew he had to watch his actions. She was still traumatized, obviously.

He couldn't help himself and googled the Greenville High Football Team as soon as possible. Sure enough, John Stevens was still head coach, and he was married to Eleanor Stevens. The picture of the couple on the school's Facebook page at a recent Homecoming Dance told him it was definitely Penny's mom. It had filled him with rage, knowing she was living right in the same town with them. First chance he got, he would take her away from there and move her into his cabin.

He shook his head and let out a grunt. He said he would take things slow, but what was he doing now? He was being a possessive ass. Even though he wanted to go at light speed, he had to slow down. His bear was insistent, though, pushing him to claim her as his mate.

At least it wasn't being belligerent, not since last night. It was ready to tear Luke into pieces for touching Penny, but as soon as she came between them, it backed down. Then, it got him thinking: Penny was the solution to soothe his bear. Or maybe, just maybe, he had it all wrong. Maybe there was no bad blood in him, and he just needed a mate.

He reached East Community Housing in no time, and as he pulled up in front of Penny's trailer, he cleared his mind. He had to make a good impression and make Penny realize that they were meant to be together, their pasts be damned.

Ben hopped out of his Jeep but not before grabbing the

dozen red roses he had picked up at the flower shop during lunch time. He walked up to her door, then pressed the doorbell. With his enhanced senses, he could hear her cute, nervous squeak, and then approaching footsteps before she opened the door.

"Hi." She looked up at him with her shy smile and pushed a curl behind her ear.

"Hi." He hoped his mouth wasn't hanging open as he stared at her. Penny looked gorgeous. Her hair was shiny and smelled fruity, the curls cascaded down her shoulders. Her skin was smooth and perfect, and he remembered how it had felt against his palm. And her lips—plump and red. He could still feel how soft her lips were and remember the taste of her —sweet, like honey. He hadn't wanted to stop when she asked him to kiss her, but he was getting overwhelmed. It took all his strength not to open the door and pull her onto his lap last night.

"Ben?"

"You look beautiful." A blush stained her cheeks. "And these are for you."

Her dark, jade-colored eyes widened. "Oh. You shouldn't have." She accepted them with a grateful nod. "Let me put these away." She turned and disappeared into the other room, probably the kitchen, then came back, the roses already in a glass vase. She set it down on the coffee table and smoothed her hands down her front.

"You didn't say where we were going, so I hope I dressed okay."

"Like I said, you look beautiful." She was wearing a green turtleneck sweater that matched her eyes and clung to her curves in a way that made his mouth water. The jeans molded to her delicious plump ass, and he had to keep his hands to his side to stop himself from reaching out and—

"Well, if you say so. Where are we going anyway?"

"To my favorite place." He led her out of the house and to the Jeep, placing his palm on the small of her back. *Slow, take it slow*, he reminded himself.

The drive back to Blackstone was quiet, with only the sound of the radio filling the air between them. It wasn't uncomfortable, though. Once in a while, he would glance over at Penny, watching her watching the outside, wondering what was on her mind.

"Oh," she said when they pulled up in front of Rosie's.

"Er, yeah." He rubbed the back of his head with his palm. "So, this is my favorite place, which is why I was here last night." He cleared his throat, slipped out, then went over to her side to open the door. "My mom brought me here all the time when I was a kid. It hasn't changed one bit. It's not fancy or anything, but the food is good."

He helped her out and then led her to the entrance. The smell of fresh pastry hit his nose, bringing back all the good memories from his childhood when he came here with his mom and dad, and later, his cousins and friends.

"Smells amazing," Penny said.

"I know, right?"

"Well, if it isn't Benjamin Walker." The woman who approached them smiled warmly. "I haven't seen you here in a while."

"Hey, Rosie," he greeted. "Yeah, I've been busy, sorry about that."

Rosie looked exactly as he remembered growing up—bright red hair and a white apron over one of the fifties-style dresses she loved wearing. She was one of those women who never seemed to age. "And who's this?" she asked.

"This is Penny. Penny Bennet," he introduced. "My date."

"A date? You've never brought a date here before." Rosie's eyes sparkled. "Unless you count his mom," she stage-whispered to Penny, which made her giggle. "Well, let's get you settled. Booth okay?"

"Sure, Rosie. Thank you."

Rosie led them to a booth by the window, which looked out onto Main Street. "Now, I hope you're not going to press your nose up against my display case tonight." She pointed to the large glass case of pies by the counter.

"I haven't done that since I was twelve," Ben said with a chuckle. Penny laughed, too.

"Only because you probably memorized my menu by then. So, how about my dinner special? Chicken pot pie with salad or soup, plus your choice of dessert. The pies are just coming out of the oven, if you don't mind waiting a bit."

Ben looked at Penny. "That sounds wonderful," she said. "Salad for me."

"I'll have the same."

Rosie nodded. "Coming right up."

"This is really nice," Penny said. "Thank you for bringing me here."

"I'm sorry I didn't think of going anywhere fancy." He frowned. "There's that new French place that just opened up."

"Oh no! I'd much rather come here. It's more special since it's your favorite place." She gasped, then blushed. "I mean, not that I think this date is special or anything."

"It is," he quickly said. "Trust me, it is."

"Will you tell me about yourself?" she asked all of a sudden. "I mean, I hardly know anything about you."

"Sure," he said. "I'm not good at talking about myself, but you can ask me anything."

"So," she began. "You work in the mines? What do you do?"

"Well, I believe, technically, my title is Vice President of Mining Operations." He chuckled. "But that's just a fancy way of saying I get stuff done up there. Basically, a chief foreman of sorts. I take care of the production schedules and day-to-day stuff."

"Do you like it? Why did you choose to go there?"

"Yeah, sure I do. It's kind of a family tradition." The confused look on her face was adorable, so he continued to explain. "My dad was foreman before me, and his dad was before him, and his dad before that. In fact, my great-great-great-great grandfather Eustace Walker was the first ever foreman of the mines when his cousin Lucas Lennox started it back in the day. His mother and Lucas' father were brother and sister. She was a dragon who married a Walker bear."

"So, Matthew and Jason and Sybil aren't really your cousins?"

"Technically, no. We're far removed, but my side of the family has always stayed here in Blackstone with the Lennoxes. I've got relatives up in Morgan Valley, and my dad and I visit them from time to time."

"That's nice."

"Yeah, I haven't visited the clan since I came back from college. I went to Colorado State to study Mining Engineering, then came right back here. Of course, I'd been working at the mines during summer vacations since I was sixteen. We all did, me, Jason, Matthew, Nathan, and Luke."

"You all grew up together?"

"Yeah, we were the best of friends."

"Sound nice," she said, then took a sip of her water.

He cleared his throat. "Well, I've been yammering here for a bit. Why don't you tell me about Houston? You said you went to live with your grandmother there?"

For a moment, he thought asking about her past would make her sad again, but her eyes lit up with the mention of her grandmother. "Yeah, she was my daddy's momma. I wasn't sure what to expect when I went to live with her, but she welcomed me with open arms.

"You never saw her before that?"

She shook her head. "No. My daddy came out here to find work and then … they just lost touch. She thought he was dead, so she was surprised to find out she had a granddaughter."

"What was she like?"

Penny smiled fondly. "She was a tough old bird. Didn't take shit from anyone, not even because she was old." She laughed. "Actually, I think she mouthed off because she was old and everyone let her get away with it. She told people what was on her mind and didn't care what they thought."

"But she was nice to you?"

"Yeah. She took care of me but never coddled me. Treated me like I was … normal." She paused and dropped her lashes, quickly looking away from him. "I can't believe she's gone. She was vibrant, all the way 'till the end, you know? She went to bed and just never woke up."

Her sadness seemed to weigh down her shoulders, and he quickly reached across the table to cover her hand with his. "I'm sorry. For your loss."

She looked up at him, her face pale and eyes wide. "Thank you."

Her skin was soft under his palm, and her hand so small

and delicate. He tried not to get too distracted. "So, is that why you came back?"

"Sort of. Mostly it was because my dad was dying. Liver cirrhosis," she explained. "The doctors said it was a wonder it didn't take him sooner. I got the call a couple of days after Grams' funeral. I couldn't stay in Houston. Her landlord had been looking for an excuse to kick her out all those years and now that she was gone, he was going to sell to some big developer. He started raising the rents to force everyone out."

"That's terrible."

She shrugged and pulled her hand away. "That's life. So, I came back, took care of my dad until he passed. He owned the trailer and left it to me, so at least I don't have to worry about rent. Although—" She quickly shut her mouth and looked out of the window. Ben probably didn't want to hear about her troubles with her dad's medical debt.

Before he could say anything, Rosie came by with their food. "Here you go, honey," she said, sliding a plate in front of Penny. "And for you." Rosie gave him a wink. He laughed when he saw she had put four pot pies on his plate. He was a shifter after all and ate twice as much as humans.

"This smells incredible," Penny said to Rosie.

"It even tastes good," she joked before sauntering away.

"Hmmm, I haven't had Rosie's pot pie in a while," Ben said as he dug into the flaky crust with his fork. He took a large chunk and put it in his mouth. The pastry melted on his tongue and the roast chicken and potatoes were tasty.

Penny was finishing her first bite, too. "Oh wow. I can see why you like it here. This is incredible."

A small bit of pastry had stuck to her upper lip, and her pink tongue darted out of her mouth to lick it off. He was so transfixed at the sight that he forgot the right way to swallow and a big chunk of crust got stuck in his throat.

"Ben!" she cried when he began to cough. "Are you okay?"

He grabbed the glass of water and swallowed a long gulp, until he was sure his throat was clear. "Yeah ... sorry ... went down the wrong pipe."

"Yeah, that can happen," she said with a chuckle.

They continued their meal, making some more small talk. He asked her about her job at The Den, and he told her stories about growing up with his friends. Rosie came by to clean their plates, and Penny ordered a slice of apple pie for dessert, while he got sweet potato and chocolate cream pie.

Penny pushed her nearly empty dessert plate away. "I honestly can't eat anymore. This was all so good."

"Glad you liked it," he said, as he finished off the last bite of sweet potato pie. "How about a bite of chocolate cream pie?" He put a small piece on his fork and offered it to her.

She eyed his fork. "Well, since you offered ...." She placed her hands on the table and pulled herself up, then leaned over to take the bite. He was staring at her lips and tongue again, thankful that he didn't have any food in his mouth. When she let out a satisfied moan, however, the sound went straight to his cock and instantly made him hard. He muttered a curse and willed himself to calm down.

"Everything okay, Ben?" she asked.

"Yeah ... just got another piece of crust stuck in my throat." He took another swig of water.

"This was really delicious. Thank you, Ben," she said.

"I'm glad you liked it."

"The company was good, too." Another blush stained her cheeks. "I hate to be the one to say it, but I should get going or I'll be late."

"Oh yeah." Where had the time gone? "I'll take you to work and wait until you're done so I can take you home."

"You don't have to do that," she said.

"I kind of have to, don't I? I mean, you didn't bring your car."

"Oh, right." She chuckled. "I'm so sorry, I didn't think about that! I guess you can come back later."

"I'll stay," he said.

"But Tim said—"

"We're good, Tim and I." Just that morning, he had gone to Tim personally to apologize and explain what had happened. Being a shifter himself, Tim accepted his explanation as to why his bear went crazy that night those men hurt Penny. *But if you do it again, you're banned for life, mate or not,* Tim had warned.

"That's nice. I'm glad you can come back to The Den now." She stood up and excused herself. While she was in the ladies' room, Ben paid for the check.

They bid Rosie goodbye, and Penny promised she'd come back for sure to try more pies. He helped her up into his Jeep, and soon they were on their way to The Den.

"You really don't have to stay," she said as they pulled into the parking lot. "You can go home. I'm sure I can ask someone for a ride."

"Nah, I got you here and I'm getting you back." Besides, this date wasn't over. He didn't want it to be over. Plus, it would be a good excuse to watch over Penny while she worked. He knew most of the shifter patrons in there wouldn't try anything, but if any more of her 'old friends' showed up, he wanted to be there. It still made his blood boil, thinking of that night, but he controlled his temper and his bear.

"I'll see you later," she said as she hopped out of his car, then strolled toward the door in the back of the building marked 'Employees Only.' He maneuvered the car into the main parking lot, pulling into the first spot by the door. It was still early and The Den wasn't open yet, so he waited inside the Jeep, checking his messages on his phone.

A movement outside caught his eye, and he snapped his head up. An unsettled feeling washed over him, and his bear suddenly reared up inside him, rattled and uneasy. He rolled the windows down and stuck his head out but saw nothing. He shook his head. *Must have been my imagination.*

Finally, the neon sign over The Den lit up and he knew they were open. He got out, locked the car, and headed inside.

Tim was standing by the bar. The older man shot him a warning look before giving him a nod. Ben walked to his favorite table and sat down, keeping an eye out for Penny.

"What can I get you, honey?"

He didn't hear the waitress approach, which was unusual. Of course, when he got a whiff of fur, he realized she was a shifter, too. *Bear*, he recognized, though he'd never seen her before. "Just a beer," he said with a cursory glance at her.

"Coming right up, honey," she said before sauntering away.

When she came back a few minutes later with his beer, she leaned down, close enough to brush her breasts against his arm. "Anything else?" She was so near, he could smell her sticky perfume and fur.

"No, I'm fine," he said, moving away from her and her cloying scent.

"Are you *sure*, hon?" She bent down so he could see the hint of cleavage as she used her upper arms to push out her breasts.

He let out an annoyed grunt and looked at her. Sure, she

was pretty, with her dark hair and red pouty lips, but she was getting on his nerves. His bear was not too happy either, and it fumed each time she got too near. Couldn't she feel it? "Yes, that's it. I'll call you if I need anything else."

She gave a pout and then walked away, swaying her hips in an exaggerated manner which might have been seductive. It's not that she wasn't attractive; he just wasn't into it. He'd had his share of women over the years; even had a serious girlfriend for a year back in college though they broke up right before graduation. But now that he had met Penny, it was like other women didn't even appeal to him.

Ah speaking of which .... He spotted her right away as she exited the employees' door by the bar. His bear perked up happily at the sight of her, and he put all thoughts of the other waitress away. Penny had changed into her uniform shirt and jeans, and she waved shyly at him as she walked across the room. He considered sitting in her section, but he didn't want her waiting on him.

As the night wore on, The Den started to fill up. He nursed his beer and got up to order another one at the bar when he was done so he didn't have to call that waitress. A couple of people stopped by to say hi and chat, mostly people he knew from town or the mines. He talked with them but kept a close eye on Penny. Thankfully, there was no trouble, and all her customers seemed to treat her with respect. Tim did run a tight ship and didn't tolerate any bullshit, but he couldn't control who came into his bar.

Closing time didn't come soon enough. Ben waited for the last patron to leave, paid his tab, and went to the parking lot. He drove his Jeep over to the employee entrance to wait for Penny.

There was that feeling again, like someone was watching

him. As he stood outside, he glanced around. A movement along the trees caught his eye. He wanted to brush it off; maybe it was a raccoon or a stray dog. As he was about to walk over and investigate, he saw Penny come through the door with Heather, the bartender. She waved goodbye to the other woman before walking over to him.

"Everything okay?" she asked as he opened the door for her.

"Sure," he said, taking one last glance at the trees in the distance. His instincts weren't screaming yet, but alarm bells were definitely raised. He filed it away in the back of his mind for now.

Their conversation was light as they drove back to Greenville. Ben asked Penny more questions about her job and what she liked to do, and she responded positively, asking him her own questions.

"I had a good time tonight. The date, anyway, not the work part," she said as he walked her up to her front door.

"Me too," he said.

They stood there for a moment, not saying anything.

"Pen—"

"I—"

She put her hand over her mouth, and he scratched the back of his neck.

"Sorry, I—"

"You go—"

This time, she laughed. "Okay, you go first."

His heart thumped in his chest. "I said we'd take it slow and we could go at your own pace and I would never do anything without asking. So," he cleared his throat, "may I kiss you, Penny?"

Her lips curled into a smile. "I thought you'd never ask."

Ben didn't wait any longer. He placed his hands tentatively on her hips, leaned down to touch his lips to hers, then covered her mouth. Willing himself to be gentle, he drank in her taste and sweet scent. It took all his self-control to stay steady, but when she let out a low moan and parted her lips, it was like a dam broke loose in him.

He pushed her back against the door, his lips never leaving hers. His mouth devoured hers, and she responded eagerly. Dipping his tongue into her mouth, he tasted her, and she was even more delicious than he'd imagined. Her small palms landed on his chest, moving up higher until her fingers dug into his shoulders.

Her innocent touch sent his cock throbbing, and he moved his hands up to cup her breasts. Goddamn, her tits were amazing, overflowing in his hands. He pressed his hips to hers, so she could feel how hard he was, trapping her between him and the door. She whimpered against his mouth and her body froze.

"Shit." He pulled away from her. "I'm sorry. That was too much."

Penny's face was flush; her green eyes stared right at him. She huffed out a breath. "I ... I haven't ... been with anyone."

"I know," he said. She was a virgin. He thought that might have been the case but didn't assume. The idea that she was untouched stirred up feelings inside him he didn't know how to name.

"Oh God." She hid her face in her hand. "That's so embarrassing. I can't believe—"

"Shh …," he soothed. "It's okay. It's my fault. It was too much."

She didn't say anything, just stared up at him with her pretty green eyes. He sighed. "Did you at least enjoy dinner?"

She nodded. "Thank you for tonight."

"You're welcome," he said. "Would you like to go out again?"

"I'd like that."

He let out a breath. "Good. Tomorrow? I'll pick you up same time?"

She hesitated but nodded, making the tension leave his body. He hadn't blown things yet.

"Well, I should get some rest."

"Yeah, get some sleep. You've been on your feet the whole night."

She turned and slipped her key into the lock. "Thanks again."

"Good night, Penny." He stood back and watched her disappear into her house. As soon as the lock clicked into place and he knew she was safe inside, he walked back to his car.

Ben supposed the night had gone better than he'd hoped for. He wanted Penny—of course he did—but he had to get a grip. If he lost control like that, he'd traumatize her for sure. *Never again*, he told himself. *Can't risk it.*

CHAPTER 9

"ARE YOU TIRED?" Ben asked as they drove away from The Den.

"Huh?" Penny turned her head toward him.

"You seem quiet," he observed.

"I'm not," she said in a defensive tone, then sank back into the seat. "Maybe a little." The truth was Penny *was* tired. Tired of wondering when Ben Walker was going to make *any* kind of move on her.

They'd gone on five dates total now. Every day, he'd pick her up, they'd go to dinner, and he'd drive her to work. He would stay the whole night, keeping a respectful distance while she was on her shift. By the time she clocked out, he'd be waiting outside to take her home. When they reached her house, he would walk her up to her door and then ... that was it. He'd say goodnight and wait until she got inside and locked the door before leaving.

Ugh. She couldn't believe she was annoyed at him for being a nice guy. And Ben was so nice to her. He opened doors, paid for their meals, and even brought her flowers. Every single date without fail. But ….

But what? Most girls complained about dates being too grabby, right? Penny pouted. Of course she'd be the one who would complain about a date not trying to cop a feel. Just her luck.

Maybe it's because you're a virgin. She squashed the thought that seemingly came from nowhere. Oh God, she told him, too, after that first date. She slapped her hand on her forehead with a loud smack.

"Penny?" Ben glanced over at her. "You all right?"

She gave him a weak smile. "I'm fine."

No, she knew why he was avoiding getting physical with her. It was that kiss. Oh God, she shivered when she thought of that amazing kiss. It was perfect. Ben. His lips. His hands. And then … she felt his erection pressing against her. It had excited her and thrilled her; she didn't know what to do. So she tensed up and froze.

He must have thought she was scared. That she had been thinking about what happened in the past. But it wasn't her fault. Over and over again, Marian said it wasn't her fault. Grams said it wasn't her fault. She knew that now.

The memories of John's attack hadn't faded away, and sometimes she had bad episodes, like when that one customer had cornered her or when Christina brought it up. However, she didn't stay a virgin because she couldn't have sex. She went on a couple of dates back in Houston. Really, she tried. But before it could go any further, she would push them away. Maybe it was partly the memories. But now she realized none of them *felt right*.

Ben did, though. Oh God, did he feel so right. But how was she supposed to tell him that?

"We're here," he announced as he opened the door.

Penny didn't even realize they had arrived. She took his hand as he helped her down. He had even installed one of those power step boards on his Jeep so she didn't have to climb up so high.

I'm an awful, awful person, she moaned to herself. Ben was the nicest guy, and she was annoyed he hadn't even tried to kiss her since their first date.

"Well, here we are," she said as they stood in front of her door.

"Uh, yeah." He seemed nervous. "So, Penny, I need to ask you something."

Yes! Oh yes, you can come in, she wanted to scream. She pursed her lips instead. "What is it?"

"Will you come to the wedding with me next week? Christina and Jason's wedding, I mean?"

"Huh?" She frowned. "I … I don't know. I mean, I know we've been going on dates, but … the wedding?"

He looked crestfallen. "Oh."

"Wait, it's not that I don't want to!" Though the thought of showing up at such a major event on Ben's arm was making the butterflies in her stomach flutter again. "I just don't have anything to wear. I don't own any fancy gowns."

"It's not white tie or anything," he said. "But I guess us guys will be wearing tuxes."

"Oh." Her heart fell. She didn't even have anything suitable for business casual. "Ben, that's nice of you to invite me. But—"

"If it's the dress that's a problem, I'll take care of it."

"Absolutely not." She was putting her foot down at that. Even a simple dress would cost way too much. "You're not paying for a dress. I still owe you for the car."

He grunted and rubbed his hand down his face. "You don't owe me anything."

"Yes, I do!" She stamped her foot like a child, then quickly realized how immature she was being. Again, Ben was being sweet and thoughtful, but she was being stubborn. But she still had her pride after all. It was her own damn blue-collar values that made her refuse to take handouts.

"I'm sorry," he said. "It's just, it would mean a lot to me if you were there."

She let out a breath. "Look, can we talk about this another time? I'm really tired."

He nodded. "Whatever you want. Can we still have dinner tomorrow?"

"Of course." The way he looked at her—so sincere and eager to please—it made her heart wrench. She couldn't stand the thought of not seeing him for more than a day. "Actually, it's my night off, so you can come a little later? Say, six-thirty? And you won't have to stay up so late, waiting for me to finish my shift."

"I don't mind at all." His face was lit up. "See you tomorrow, then?"

"See you." She went inside, closed and locked the door behind her, and listened to Ben's heavy footsteps as they grew fainter. She smacked her forehead on the wood. *I really am an awful person.*

Penny was sitting in her kitchen the next morning, enjoying a cup of coffee and a book when she heard her cell phone ring. "Huh?" Who would call her at this time? She scrambled for her purse, which she had tossed onto the couch last night. "Hello?"

"Penny, it's me."

Ben. Oh God, did he change his mind about her? "Hey, there," she said, trying to sound casual. "Did you need to reschedule or something?"

"No, we're still on for tonight. Unless you need—"

"No! Er, I mean, I'm good."

"Good. Now, I called you because … well, don't hate me, but I kind of did something."

Penny sank down on the couch and twisted a curl of her hair in her fingers. "What do you mean?"

"Well, remember last night when you said you didn't have anything to wear to a wedding?"

"Yeah?"

"And you wouldn't let me buy you a dress?"

"Uh-huh?"

"Well, I got someone to help."

"Who?" Before Ben could answer, an insistent knock made her jump up. "Hold on." She put the phone away from her ear and bounded to the door. When she looked in the peephole, she frowned in confusion. It was Kate Caldwell, Nathan's sister. She'd met Kate twice before, once when she served them at Catherine's bachelorette party and the second time was when she walked up to Christina at the cafe. But what was she doing here?

"Kate?"

"Penny, my girl!" Kate breezed into her living room the moment she cracked the door open.

Another figure was right behind Kate. "Hey, Penny!" Sybil Lennox greeted as she followed behind Kate. Sybil was Matthew and Jason's sister, and Ben's cousin. "How are you?"

"Good. It's nice to see you, but what are you guys doing here? How did you know where I live?"

"Ben sent us!" Kate said cheerfully as she plopped herself down on the couch.

"What?"

"You're on the phone with him, right?" Kate nodded to her hand.

"Oh. Right." She put her phone up to her ear. "Ben?"

"Are they there?"

"Kate and Sybil?"

"Yeah."

"They are. But I don't understand."

"Well, you know how you didn't have anything to wear to the wedding?"

"Uh-huh?"

"I told you, they're there to help."

"I said I didn't want you to pay for a dress!" she exclaimed.

"I'm not."

"He's not," Kate piped in. She stood up and grabbed the phone from Penny. "Ben, we'll take care of this, okay … Yeah, yeah, don't worry about it. She's in good hands. Now stop moping. Bye." She rolled her eyes and passed the phone back to Penny. "Get dressed, Penny, my girl! We're going out!"

"But—"

"Go!" Kate shooed her, pushing her toward the bedroom.

Penny wanted to protest more, but she had a feeling it would do no good. She grabbed some clothes from her closet and quickly dressed.

"Where are we going?" Penny asked later as they sat in Sybil's car. They were driving in the direction of Blackstone. "I told Ben not to buy me a dress."

"He's not," Sybil said.

Penny slumped back and crossed her arms over her chest. "*You* guys are not buying me one either."

"We aren't." Kate looked back at her from the front passenger seat. "Look, Ben told us you didn't have anything to wear to the wedding and you wouldn't accept a dress from him. So, I'm taking you to a friend of mine. She's an aspiring designer and would be absolutely thrilled if you would wear one of her designs to the wedding."

Surely a dress by a designer would be out of her budget. "I can't afford it."

Kate shook her head. "You're just borrowing it. Hollywood movie stars do it all the time, you know? For exposure."

Huh. That actually wasn't a bad solution. She could keep her pride and go to the wedding with Ben. "I guess that would be okay."

"Great. You'll love her stuff. Her style's all vintage and glam."

They drove for another twenty minutes until they arrived at a house just on the edge of Blackstone. It was small but quaint, painted in blue and white. The trio walked up to the door, and Kate rang the doorbell. The door opened a few seconds later.

"Hello, Kate."

"Dutchy!" Kate greeted. "Thanks for letting us drop by on short notice."

"How could I say no to a fashion emergency?" The woman who answered was probably their age, with pale blue eyes and strawberry blond hair that was perfectly styled in waves around her face. "Come in, please." She smiled at them and stood aside to let them through.

"Guys, this is Duchess Forrester."

"Please, call me Dutchy. Everyone does."

"You already know Sybil, but this is Penny. She's the one with a fashion emergency."

"I'm sorry for the trouble," Penny said in a quiet voice.

Dutchy laughed, her voice like tinkling bells. "No trouble at all. I'm not exactly busy. Let's go into my workshop."

She led them into the main area of the one-story house, which should have been the living room, but this room was filled with half-unpacked boxes, bolts of fabric, two sewing machines, and several mannequins. The mannequins were outfitted in gorgeous outfits, from casual sundresses to an elegant-looking ball gown in black and white. "Sorry about the mess; I'm still figuring things out. I only moved in a couple of days ago."

"Oh, that's nice," Penny said, looking around her. "From where?"

"New York. I just finished fashion school and was looking for a change," she explained. "I came to visit Blackstone last month. My aunts live here, and they said I should check it out." She smiled wistfully. "I don't know, something about this place makes me feel at home."

"Dutchy is going to start her fashion line here," Kate explained. "She's going to become famous!"

"Kate, you're too kind," Dutchy said with a laugh.

"Can the modesty, sister! You're so talented. Blackstone will be the place where you flourish! I mean, imagine, a shifter designer making gowns for other shifters! You could start a trend!"

Penny didn't realize Dutchy was a shifter, though it made sense, if she felt she belonged here. The rest of the world, especially in the big cities, wasn't very welcoming to their kind.

"Blackstone is growing, so I thought, why not? Anyway,

please have a seat." She gestured to the couch, the one area that was relatively clutter-free, and sat next to Penny. "So, Kate tells me you're going to the Lennox-Stavros wedding and you need a dress."

"Yeah." Penny fidgeted with the bottom of her shirt. Dutchy looked so elegant in her vintage dress and sandals. She wished she had thrown on something more stylish than a shirt and jeans. "Kate said you'd let me borrow a dress?"

"That's the plan."

"But," she looked around at the beautiful dresses on the mannequins, "all your dresses are gorgeous. And probably expensive."

"Oh, don't worry." Dutchy put her hands over Penny's. "You'll be doing *me* a favor if you wear one of my designs to the biggest social event in Blackstone."

"You'll be a walking billboard," Kate said.

"But more elegant," Sybil added. "Just give people Dutchy's name when they ask about your dress."

"Oh, I can do that," Penny said, nodding her head excitedly.

"Great. It's settled then," Dutchy said. "I think I know the perfect one. It's an earlier work of mine, but it should still be in good condition. Give me a second." She disappeared into another section of the house and came back with a garment bag. "Here." She handed it to Penny. "Come with me."

Penny followed Dutchy to another room. She hung the dress on a coat rack in the corner. When she unzipped it, she let out a gasp. The dress was gorgeous. It had a navy blue satin corseted bodice with a sweetheart neckline. The skirt was made of layers of dark blue tulle covered in gold specks, like the night sky filled with stars. The fabric was delicate to the touch, and she ran her hands over it lovingly.

"Do you like it?" Dutchy asked.

"It's beautiful."

She gave Penny a warm smile. "Try it on then."

Penny nodded and took off her clothes. She slid the blue dress over her body and when Dutchy came forward to zip her up, another gasp left her mouth.

"Perfect fit," Dutchy said.

It really was. She could breathe in the dress and it didn't pinch or bunch anywhere.

"Let's get a better look outside."

She left the room, lifting the skirt as she walked. This was the fanciest dress she'd ever worn, and she didn't want to ruin it by tripping all over herself. "Well?" she asked Kate and Sybil when she stood in the middle of the living room.

Kate's eyes were wide and her mouth open. For once, she was actually speechless.

"Oh Penny, you look gorgeous!" Sybil said, clapping her hands together. "You'll be the most beautiful girl there."

"Aside from the bride," Penny joked.

"Seriously, Penny, you are fine," Kate said. "And I mean *fiiiiine*. All the girls will be jealous when you show up on Ben's arm. He cleans up nice too, ya know?"

"And you'll be meeting his parents," Sybil added. "But don't be nervous or anything. Aunt Laura and Uncle James are the sweetest."

Penny thought for a moment. Meeting Ben's parents would be *big*. Like, humongous. And though she was nervous, she'd be a liar if she said she didn't want it to happen.

"Don't worry, they'll love you," Kate assured her. "Especially since you're his mate and all."

Penny felt her cheeks grow hot. "He … he … told you?"

Kate grinned. "More like, I twisted his arm at work this

morning until he told me why he looked like someone had kicked his pet cat or something."

"She probably literally did," Sybil added.

"Pshaw, I did that to him all the time when we were kids. Anyway," she turned back to Penny. "He *really* wants you to come. They'll be so thrilled you'll be giving them grandkids soon."

"Yeah, well that means Ben has to have sex with me first." Penny was pretty sure she had said that in her head, not out loud. But from the shocked looks on the three other women's faces, she knew they had heard every word. *Damn word vomit!* She cringed and covered her mouth with her hands.

The silence in the room was deafening. Sybil shifted uncomfortably beside her, while Dutchy stood off to the side trying not to look at her. Of course, Kate could *only* stare, her mouth open.

"*What?*" Kate finally said. "Ben hasn't been all over *that?*"

Penny shook her head.

"Why?"

"Er…."

Kate got to her feet, throwing her hands in the air. "And why haven't you been all over him? I mean—excuse me while I push the bile down my throat because he's like a brother to me but—Ben is a smokin' specimen! You need to climb that man bear like a tree!"

"I don't know how! I've never had sex before." *Oh hell, not again.* Her face felt like a three-alarm fire.

This time, Kate's head swung back and forth between Penny and Sybil, then she burst out laughing as she fell back on the couch, clutching her stomach. "Oh. My. God!"

Sybil let out a long, drawn-out sigh. "Isn't this getting old yet?"

Kate waved at them. "You guys should form the Blackstone Virgins Club or something."

Sybil rolled her eyes and looked at Penny. "Sorry, my virginity's a running joke with her. Kate, will you stop!" Sybil said. "Penny's obviously embarrassed."

"S-s-sorry," Kate said, wiping her eyes with the back of her hand. She cleared her throat. "Sybil's been my friend since we were in diapers, so I can joke with her like that. I didn't mean to make fun of you."

"It's fine."

"But ... really?"

Penny bit her lip. "It's not that I didn't want to or tried." She swallowed the lump in her throat. "I'm just ... something happened when I was younger and since then I just ...."

Sybil put an arm around her. "Penny, I had no idea."

"*Jesus.*" Kate was gritting her teeth. "I'm sorry."

She straightened her shoulders. "It's not that I can't or don't want to. No one felt right, that's all. No one until Ben. And he won't even ... he thinks he's doing the right thing. I mean, obviously he is, but he's so nice. I just don't know what to do or what to tell him! Am I supposed to wave a flag? Take an ad out in the paper?"

"Screw Me Silly, Ben Walker!" Kate waved her hand in the air like she was reading a big headline. Even Sybil guffawed. "Aww, Penny, my girl." Kate put an arm around her. "Look, it's no big deal. You're his mate. He can only resist you for so long. It'll happen for you."

"Do you think it'll happen before the next ice age?" Penny asked wryly. "But seriously. Do you think he's turned off by the fact that I'm a virgin?"

"What? No!" Kate protested. "No way. I know Ben. I mean, not about his sex life or anything, but he's the type of person who will do the right thing. He's always been there, looking out for us and taking care of us like a big brother. He's a nice guy. And because he's a nice guy, he's going to do everything to put you first. Even if it means blue balls for the rest of his life."

Sybil swatted her on the shoulder. "Kate!"

"Ugh, c'mon, we're all adults," Kate said.

Penny sighed, her shoulders sinking low. "I don't know what to do. I like him so much."

"You have to seduce him," Dutchy said matter-of-factly. "And I know how." She disappeared into the other room again, then came back with something lacy and satiny in her hands. "Here." She held it up. It was a light pink corset and garter belt set.

"Holy. Shit." Kate exclaimed. "Ben's going to cream his pants when he sees you in that."

"It's the same size as the dress so it should fit you," Dutchy said. "Go ahead," she held it out to Penny. "It's yours."

"What? No, I can't take that! You're already letting me borrow your dress!"

"And you're giving me free advertisement. Please, just take it. It's a gift. Besides, I can't take it back after you wear it."

"Yeah, there might not be anything left," Kate said.

Penny took it gratefully. "But, so, what do I do? We're going out to dinner tonight, and he usually takes me straight home after."

"Just give him a peek of what you're wearing," Dutchy said. "Put on something really sweet and innocent on top. Then, when you're all alone, give him a preview."

Penny flushed. Could she really do that?

"And then you know what happens after, right?" Kate asked.

"Kate, I'm sure Penny knows the mechanics," Sybil said.

"Excuse me, Miss Sybil Lennox, but you've never had a first time! Penny needs to know what she's in for. Especially with Ben." Kate put her palms together and then pulled them apart in an exaggerated manner.

"Ew! Kate!" Sybil lobbed a throw pillow at her.

Kate ducked. "What? He's a shifter, so you know he's gifted in the size department!" She turned to Penny. "Seriously, you have to set the pace. Tell him to go slow. He can't go wailing on your vagina like the guitar solo from *Sweet Child O' Mine*."

Oh God, she hadn't even thought of *that*.

Dutchy laughed. "Well ladies, I think Penny's embarrassed enough. Her face is about as red as her hair."

Penny shot Dutchy a grateful look, glad that the other woman put a stop to the teasing. She was nervous enough.

They chatted for a few more minutes, and Penny exchanged numbers with Dutchy so they could arrange for her to pick up the dress after some minor adjustments. They said their goodbyes, and the three women left.

CHAPTER 10

After they dropped off Sybil at work, Kate drove Penny back home and then proceeded to help—meaning bully—her into picking out an outfit for her date with Ben. She didn't have a lot of clothes, but they ended up picking something innocent and sweet as Dutchy suggested—a white blouse and a black pencil-cut skirt.

"You look like a librarian," Kate said.

"Is that good?" Penny asked.

"He was a teenage boy. Of course it is," Kate answered.

Penny showered, and then Kate helped her into the corset. "Oh boy, I don't know how you're going to get out of this thing without Ben ripping it apart."

Her face went hot, thinking about being with Ben. Would this really work? She didn't know what she'd do if he rejected her. But Kate had said she was irresistible to him as his mate.

"Okay, Penny," Kate said, picking up her purse. "Ben should be here any minute. Put on your librarian outfit and go and get our boy!"

Penny giggled. "Thanks Kate, for everything."

They said their goodbyes and soon she was alone again. Penny finished dressing and put on her only high-heeled shoes. She was used to wearing comfy flats and sneakers because of her job, but she couldn't resist this particular pair when she was out shopping one day. They were black with skinny heels and had crisscross straps across the front. She'd never had any occasion to wear them until now. When she stood up from her bedroom to walk to the living area, she wobbled. As she crossed the room, she nearly tumbled before she reached the couch.

"Maybe I should have practiced beforehand," she said aloud. "This might not be a good idea." As she reached down to take the strap off a shoe, she heard the familiar knock. "Eeep!" Penny shot up and bolted to the door, opening it quickly. "Ben!" she said in a breathless voice.

"Hey, Penny." He flashed her a megawatt smile and held out a bunch of flowers. "Are you ready? Did you have a job interview or something?"

"Huh?" She looked down at her outfit. "Uhm … no, I just wanted to look nice." She realized she did look like she worked as a secretary at an office.

"Oh. Yeah, you do."

"Let me put those in water." As she stepped forward to grab the flowers, she forgot about the shoes and toppled forward. A soft cry escaped her mouth as she waved her arms, trying to maintain balance, but to no avail; she went crashing straight into Ben's arms.

"Whoah! You okay?" he asked as he righted her, his blue eyes staring down at her.

"Uh, yeah." She let out a giggle that sounded forced to her

ears and then kicked herself mentally. "I should change my shoes."

"No!" he said. "I mean, yeah, if you're not comfortable."

"It's fine." She turned around, hoping to hide the embarrassment on her face, and walked over to the bedroom where she changed into her more sensible flats.

"Ready?" he asked.

"Yeah."

Her first attempt at being sexy was a bust, so she only hoped the rest of this scheme would turn out better.

When they entered the cafe, they didn't even bother to wait for Rosie to bring them to a booth, but instead automatically walked to the one they always sat in. Ben usually sat on the right, facing the dining room, while she sat across from him. This time, Penny thought it would be nice to sit together, so she sat on his side.

"Did you want to switch?" Ben asked. "I guess I'm always the one looking out."

"Uhm, no, it's fine." Oh God, should she say something about wanting to sit next to him? Maybe she should have asked. What if he liked his own space? "I mean, yes! I just wanted to switch it up."

"Okay." Ben slid into the seat across from her.

Rosie came over and instead of asking them what they wanted, she just said, "The usual?"

"Yes," both of them said at the same time. Rosie nodded, but as she walked away, she winked at Penny. Did she somehow know ... Maybe Kate told her?

"Are you okay Penny? Your face just went red."

"What? Oh no, it's just too hot in here." She fanned herself with her hand.

"Weather's warming up. Looks like spring's finally coming," Ben said.

"Yeah, I'm just about done with winter," she said. "So, what do you like to do when the weather gets warm?"

"Well, I like the outdoors, so I do some fishing …."

Penny nodded and pretended to listen, but she was really trying to figure out her next move in this whole seduction thing. She was getting antsy. Maybe she should have asked the girls for more advice. They made seducing Ben sound easier than it was. Like, all she had to do was whip off her clothes. But where was she supposed to do that? In the middle of the cafe?

She'd seen some movies and read in her books about playing footsie under the table. Maybe that might work? She slipped her foot out of her shoe and stretched it toward him, hoping to brush it against his calf. But she forgot how tall he was and how long his legs were, so she ended up smacking him on the knee with her foot.

"… and then when—what the fuck?" Ben nearly jumped off his seat. "There's something under there!" He ducked his head down to try and look under the table.

Penny wanted the earth to swallow her up right then and there. Embarrassment burned her face like the heat of a thousand suns. "Sorry!" she squeaked, pulling her foot back. "I was, uh, stretching. I had a cramp in my foot."

"You should have that looked at," he said. "Those hours on your feet at your job probably aren't good for you."

"Right."

Rosie's arrival with their drinks and food saved her from

further mortification. They thanked Rosie, and Penny thanked God that Ben was distracted by the food.

"Penny? Everything okay?" Ben asked as he finished the last of his chicken pot pie.

"Huh?" She was probably staring off into the distance.

"Are you not hungry? Is the pie not good?"

She looked down at her half-eaten pie. She was too nervous to eat, not to mention the corset pushed her stomach in so tight, she was afraid it'd burst open if she had anything more than a bite. Kate had helped her put it on, and when Penny protested at the tightness, Kate said this was how it was supposed to fit.

"Um, no, it's fine!" She gave a nervous laugh. "Yeah, I'm just not hungry is all. Do you want my pie?" She winced at her choice of words.

"Really? Yeah, sure!" Ben said in an excited voice as he grabbed her plate.

Penny sighed. *Maybe I should give up.* But she almost heard Kate's voice in her head, telling her she better climb that man bear. So, she mentally squared her shoulders. "Ben?"

He looked up from the plate. "Yeah?"

"Would you mind if ... I mean." She stood up and then slid into his side of the booth. He looked at her curiously. "I was thinking ...." She reached toward him to touch his arm, but he raised his hand at the same time and ended up knocking his glass of water all over her. She let out a shriek as the cold water splashed over the front of her shirt.

"Penny! I'm sorry!"

"I'm fine!" She slid off the seat and turned around.

"Wait!"

"I said, I'm fine," she snapped and marched toward the bathroom, flinging the door open and walking inside. She braced herself on the sink and looked at herself in the mirror as she wiped the drops of water from her face.

Maybe I should give up. Ben probably changed his mind about me when he had more chances to think about it. Maybe he thinks I'm not worth the trouble but is too polite to break things off.

The door to the bathroom flew open, and she nearly jumped out of her skin.

"Penny, what's—"

Ben's eyes bulged, and his nostrils flared. "Penny." His voice went hoarse.

"Ben?"

He stepped forward, and his large frame made the small room feel even tinier. As he moved toward her, Penny found herself stepping back until she hit the tile wall behind her. His eyes darkened to a stormy blue and made a thrill rush down her spine, straight into her gut. She lowered her lashes.

"What are you wearing?" he asked.

"Huh?" She whipped her head up. His jaw was tense and his face inscrutable.

"Under your shirt." His gaze drifted below her chin.

Penny looked down. The water made the white shirt transparent and caused it to stick to her chest. The pink and black lace was evident underneath as were the curves of her breasts thrusting up.

He let out a small growl, and another shiver went through her. But instead of feeling embarrassed, she was emboldened. Her heart pounded in her chest and her fingers trembled as she began to unbutton the blouse. The damp fabric fell from her shoulders, revealing the corset underneath.

"Why are you wearing that?" he asked in a husky voice.

She murmured under her breath.

"Say it louder." He tipped her chin with a finger. "Tell me."

"I wanted to seduce you."

His eyes blazed, and his pupils contracted. "Seduce me?"

She nodded. "You've just been so nice and respectful. I wasn't sure if you wanted me."

"You think I don't want you?" Ben ran a hand through his hair. "I'm going crazy from wanting you."

"Then why haven't you tried to kiss me again? Or tried anything more?"

"Penny, I wanted to take it slow."

"Because of what happened to me?"

He nodded. "I practically mauled you in front of your door. You tensed up, and I knew it was too much. So, I thought I would give it some time."

"That night?" *Oh.* "Ben, no! I tensed up because I'd never felt like that before." She let out a long breath. "Every other guy I tried to date, I would push them away. It didn't feel right. *They* didn't feel right." She searched his face, trying to gauge his reaction. "But when you kissed me that night, I don't know what it was. Maybe it's because of what you said. About being mates."

"You tensed up because you liked it?"

"I know it seems strange, but yeah. I was surprised. You didn't feel like anyone else. Ben." She touched his arm; his muscles jumped underneath her palm. "You say I'm yours, but I think … you're mine, too."

He sucked in a breath. "Penny …."

In half a second, his lips were on hers. And he wasn't soft or gentle. Oh no. Ben was rough, urgent, and insistent. It made her toes curl and excitement lurch within her.

He urged her mouth open. When she obliged, his tongue dipped between her lips, teasing her. She opened to him eagerly, wanting to taste more of him. His hand slipped under her skirt and brushed against the lace of the stockings and garter belt. He pulled back, his mouth a millimeter from hers.

"What else are you wearing?" he asked in a rough voice, his warm breath tickling her swollen lips.

"Why don't you see for yourself?" She raised the skirt high enough to reveal the lace band around her thigh and the strap of the garter belt.

"Hot damn," he cursed, before planting another kiss on her mouth. "I can't wait. Let's go."

"Where?" she asked breathlessly.

"Home. My cabin, I mean." He unbuttoned his plaid shirt, tossed it around her, then grabbed her hand and dragged her out of the bathroom. She nearly tripped as they walked across the cafe, but somehow kept up with his longer strides. They were out of the restaurant and halfway to the car when he stopped and let out a frustrated breath.

Did he change his mind? "Ben?"

He turned to her. "Sorry. Won't be long. I forgot to pay." He reached for his wallet then stopped halfway, his brows knitting together.

She turned her head back to the cafe. Rosie was standing by the window, a piece of white paper in her hand. With a sly smile, she tore up the check and waved them away.

Ben gave Rosie a grateful nod, then rushed Penny into his Jeep, practically tossing her inside as he opened the door and lifted her into the seat. Soon, they were driving out of Blackstone, toward the main road that led up the mountain. Penny realized she didn't even know where he lived, but it didn't matter. She knew she would be safe, as long as she was with Ben.

Ben looked ahead, concentrating on the road as he maneuvered the vehicle up the winding highway. She watched his strained expression, wondering what he was thinking. He was only wearing a white undershirt, and his muscles tensed as he turned the wheel with the road. Hoping to soothe him, she reached out to touch his arm. When he winced and flinched away, she shrank back.

He glanced over at her and frowned. "Sorry, it's not you."

"Huh?"

His shoulders tensed visibly. "Penny, I want you so fucking bad, if you touch me right now, I swear you're going to find yourself in the backseat with your legs in the air so fast, it'll make your head spin." He stared ahead. "I don't want that. Not for our first time."

"Oh." Penny shivered, thinking of the visual in her head. Flat on her back, legs in the air. Ben on top of her. God, the thought made her ache, and she could feel the wetness pooling between her legs.

"Penny," he warned. "I can smell you, too."

"Oh. Sorry."

He laughed. "Don't be sorry, sweetheart. Never be sorry for that."

They drove for what seemed like forever. The anticipation in her veins made her antsy. It felt like they were never going to get there. When he stopped the car and killed the engine, she didn't bother to wait for him to get the door. She opened it and stepped out on her own.

"Holy …." She looked at the 'cabin' and then at Ben, who cocked his head to the side. "Ben, this isn't a cabin."

"Huh?"

"You said you lived in a cabin."

"It's made of logs," he said. "And is in the middle of the woods."

"Ben, this is a *mansion*." She gestured to the two-story building with the stonework wraparound porch. "It's huge."

"I like my space." He shrugged. "C'mon."

He took her hand and led her up to the porch and to the front door. When they entered and he turned on the lights, her eyes bugged out of their sockets. It was just as luxurious inside—high vaulted ceilings, exposed stone, matching wooden details. There was a fireplace in the living area and a large sectional leather couch. The decor was masculine and tasteful at the same time. Her entire trailer could fit in this main room. Heck, it could fit four of her trailers.

"Penny?"

"Sorry," she mumbled. "Your place is really nice."

"Yeah, my dad helped me design it, and my mom did the interior."

"Oh, that's nice. Your mom is really talented. Does she work as an interior designer? It's—"

"Penny?"

"Huh?"

"I don't really want to talk about my mom right now."

"Oh. Right. Gotcha. Hey!"

He swept her up into his arms, as if she were weightless, then marched up the long, wooden staircase that led to the second floor. She clung to him, wrapping her arms around his neck and laying her head on his chest. His body was so warm and hard, so different from hers. And yet it felt so right to be here with him.

Ben walked into the bedroom on the opposite end of the long hallway. It was dark inside, with only the dim moonlight coming in from the enormous picture window on one side. She felt him lower her down onto something soft and then a lamp to her right clicked on, revealing his handsome face.

He placed a hand on her cheek. "Just tell me if I'm going too fast," he said. "You can say stop any time."

She smiled up at him and nodded, making him sigh in relief. "Do you want to see what I'm wearing underneath?"

His eyes darkened and a muscle in his jaw ticked. "Yes."

She unwrapped the shirt he had thrown on her. It was so warm and smelled so delicious, so like him that she was reluctant to take it off. But she knew it was worth it when she saw his reaction.

"Show me more," he said, his eyes roving over her body.

Penny swung her legs over the side of the bed. He backed up a bit to give her space as she stood up and reached behind her to unzip the skirt. She let it pool at her ankles. The black stockings went halfway up her thighs and were held up by the garter belt connected to the corset.

"Jesus," he growled. "You're perfect." Ben lowered his head to take her mouth, moving over it with a savage mastery that made her feel dizzy. "Sorry," he murmured against her lips, then smothered them again with his.

Sorry for what? The ripping sound of fabric answered her question, and the corset fell away from her torso as he impatiently shoved it down to her waist.

His hands felt like a brand as they landed on her bare skin. He pushed her down on the bed, planting her on the mattress as he knelt in front of her and nudged her legs apart, pushing between them.

She moaned against his mouth as he pressed his torso to her; her thighs tightened around him in response. His chest was rock hard, and she couldn't help herself. She held onto his muscled shoulders, squeezing them and digging her fingers into them as he continued to ravage her mouth.

She whimpered when he pulled away, but the trail of heat

he left as his lips dragged down her throat made her moan and grip his shoulders harder. Oh God, his mouth. Warm and wet as it enclosed over a nipple. His tongue lazily circled the bud, the rough pad sweeping against it like sweet torture.

His hand reached up to cup her other breast, his thumb brushing over the nipple. She squeezed her thighs around him harder, unaware that she was rocking her hips against him until he groaned and pushed her down on the bed and farther up so she was in the middle with her back on the mattress.

Ben got up, his eyes raking over her half-naked body as he took his shirt off, unbuckled his belt, and shucked his pants down, leaving him only in his underwear. She stared at him, unable to drag her gaze away from his muscled chest and arms, his perfect eight-pack abs, and the trail of hair that disappeared under his boxer briefs. Shyly, she lowered her lashes, but not before she got a peek at the significant bulge between his legs.

He tore what remained of the corset away, leaving her only in her panties and stockings. Spreading her thighs apart, he moved between them, lowering his head until—

There was more ripping as he turned her lace panties into scraps. His mouth finally made contact with her naked core. "Ben!" The press of his mouth on her made her flood with wetness and seemed to urge him on. His tongue darted out to lick up her juices, driving her wild.

She grabbed at his hair, twisting the locks as he continued to feast on her. The pressure building was too much, and she closed her eyes, her vision bursting to white as her body tensed and then electricity arced through her. She lifted her hips off the mattress, pressing up against his talented tongue as mind-numbing pleasure spread over her.

"Oh. God." She panted as she came back down and her

eyes flew open. It was unlike anything she'd ever felt before. She looked down, her face aflame when their eyes clashed.

"Did you …?"

She nodded, and he gave her a feral smile as he crawled over her. The hairs on his chest tickled her stomach and breasts and she squirmed, then sighed when he gently kissed her. He caressed her face with his calloused fingers, touching her jaw, her neck, trailing a path between her breasts and down her stomach.

Fingers skimmed over her swollen and wet center. She gasped as he pressed one digit in her tightness; her body tensed.

"Relax, sweetheart," he whispered. "You'll have to relax."

"I'll try," she said.

He dipped a finger deeper, and then added another. He stroked her inner walls, and she found her hips moving in rhythm with his fingers. He urged her on with sweet, gentle words, and soon, her body was exploding in another orgasm as he continued to tease her.

Ben kissed her on the mouth. "That's it sweetheart. You're nice and wet for me." He reached down between them, and she watched as he hooked a thumb in his waistband and pulled down his underwear.

She couldn't help herself and let out a gasp. How on earth was he going to—

"It's okay," he assured her as he removed the boxer briefs entirely. "We'll go slow."

She nodded in agreement, her throat too dry to say anything. He reached over to the side, taking something out of the night stand. Unwrapping the foil packet, he took out the condom and rolled it over his thick cock.

"Are you sure, Penny?" he asked.

"Yes," she said, her voice hardly shaking. She had never been more sure of anything else in her entire life.

Ben moved between her legs. "You're so beautiful like this, Penny. Your skin is so soft and smooth." He leaned down and kissed her neck, moving to the tops of her breasts. "Your hair smells so good and looks so good when it's spread like this on my pillow." He ran his fingers through her hair. "I've been thinking and dreaming of you in my bed since I met you."

"You have?"

He nodded. "Penny, I want you to be mine."

"Then make me yours."

He sucked in a breath as he moved his hips toward her. She felt the blunt tip of his cock nudging against her. Though her instinct was to close her legs, she resisted and relaxed her body.

"Penny," he growled as he paused.

"Don't stop."

Ben pushed, slowly filling her. She held her breath as the brief pain made her wince, and she bit the inside of her cheek to keep from crying out. He moaned her name and turned her head so he could kiss her. She sighed against his lips, allowing him to comfort her as the pain subsided.

She opened her eyes. He looked strained, his eyes closed and his brows furrowed. "Ben." She touched his brow, and he relaxed. He looked down at her, the expression on his face tender.

"Are you okay?" he asked.

She smiled and nodded. "Yes."

"I can—Penny!" He let out a guttural sound as she pushed up her hips, clenching around him. "God, you feel amazing." He moved inside her, and she inhaled a quick breath and grabbed at his shoulders.

"*Ben.*"

It was as if his name on her lips was too much. He cradled her in his arms as he began to move. Slow, tentatively at first.

Pleasure zinged through her body with each drag of his cock inside her. She grasped at him, her body moving and keeping in time. He mouthed at her neck, finding that sweet spot beneath her ear that she didn't know existed. "Oh!" she cried when his tongue licked at it, and then his mouth sucked at her flesh. It seemed to double the sensations, and it was like her body was one big pleasure zone. "Ben!" she cried again as she moved her hips. "More."

He grunted and slipped a hand under her buttocks, cupping her and moving her closer. When he changed his angle, she could feel him hit her clit just right and she exploded in another orgasm, surprising even herself as the pure pleasure took over her body.

She relaxed, feeling like she was floating on air. Ben didn't slow down however, and soon, her body was tensing again. "Oh. God."

Ben gripped her tighter, pulling her up to him as he groaned. He pushed into her, and she felt his cock throb inside her. She shivered as a smaller orgasm pulsed though her. She wrapped her legs around him as if she was afraid to let go.

He relaxed against her. There was something so intimate about having his weight on her. She wanted to stay like this for a long time. She sighed and pressed a kiss to his shoulder.

"Penny." He brushed the hair off her cheek. "Are you okay?"

He looked down at her with such concern it made her heart swell. "I am now," she said with a weak smile.

"Good." He kissed her cheek. Bracing his arms on either

side of her as he lifted himself off, he carefully pulled out of her. "Hold on." He slid off the bed and disappeared into the bathroom. Moments later, he came back with a small towel in his hand. "This should help." He pressed it against her core and she sighed. The towel was warm and wet and brought some relief to the slight ache there.

"Thank you," she said, then gently pushed his hand away.

"I'm sorry," he said. "For the pain."

"Don't be." She reached up to cup his cheek, his thick beard tickling her palm. "It was great. All of it."

His face looked relieved. "It was for me, too." He leaned down to give her a tender kiss. "Will you stay the night?"

"But don't you have work tomorrow?"

"We can leave early, and I'll drop you off at home." He was already pulling the covers down, urging her to join him under the blanket.

"All right." She slid under the covers and then settled against him, laying her head on his chest.

"Are you sleepy at all?"

She shook her head. "I'm used to late nights."

"I'm usually asleep by ten," he confessed. "We have early days at the mines."

"But you've been staying up to take me home this week," she exclaimed. "Oh no! I'm—"

"Shh." He stroked a hand down her naked back. "It's all right. It was worth it. Besides, it's more of a habit than a need. I don't need all that sleep," he assured her. "If you're not sleepy, it's okay. You can watch TV," he nodded to the remote on the nightstand, "or read or something. Just stay with me tonight."

"Of course," she said. "Get some sleep."

She waited until he closed his eyes, then snuggled deeper

against him. A sigh escaped her mouth. This was all so new to her, but in a good way. She never thought cuddling with anyone could be so nice. But now, pressed up against Ben's body and feeling the rise and fall of his chest as his breathing evened, she felt content for the first time in her life.

CHAPTER 11

THE LIGHT HITTING his closed lids woke Ben up. It was a strange sensation because he was usually up before dawn. When he cracked an eye open and saw the early morning light filtering through the window in his bedroom, he realized he had slept in.

A sense of urgency rushed through him, but when he felt Penny's soft body against his, he relaxed. He stroked her back to remind himself she was real. This was real. He really did make love to her last night, and now she was in his bed, her head on his chest and an arm thrown across him. When was the last time he slept so soundly? Months maybe. If it wasn't his bear keeping him up, it was his own dark thoughts. But, maybe, those were behind him now.

She looked so peaceful, with her eyes closed and her lips slightly parted. He didn't want to disturb her, but he had to call work. His phone was right on the nightstand, and he reached for it.

Ben frowned. There were no notifications. He was

expecting at least a dozen. He quickly sent off a text to Nathan.

Sorry, slept in. Be there in 20.

The reply came in a second.

Don't worry about it. Take your time. Kate explained and told me not disturb you this morning if I wanted to keep my balls.

He bit his lip to stifle a laugh.

Thanks for holding down the fort. I'll let you know when I'm on my way.

Nathan replied with, *Enjoy your morning,* followed by an emoji of a thumbs up, an eggplant and water droplets.

He chuckled. Nathan was an asshole, but a lovable one.

"Ben?" Penny's eyes fluttered open, then she raised her head. "Ben! It's morning! You're late for work."

"It's okay," he soothed, rubbing her shoulder. "Nathan's taking care of things at the mines."

She let out a sigh of relief. "I hope you don't get in trouble."

"I'm the boss, remember?" He laughed. "I'll just get a bit of ribbing."

"Oh."

"But it'll be worth it because I got to see how beautiful you look while you're asleep."

A pretty blush spread over her cheeks.

"And while you're awake, too." He hooked an arm under her and pulled her on top of him, then planted a kiss on her mouth.

She responded eagerly, squirming on top of him, her tits rubbing against his chest and her hips moving against his. His cock was hard in an instant, and he groaned when the tip brushed against her luscious thighs.

"Sorry," he said as he pulled away. "You must be sore."

Penny shook her head, her wild coppery curls bouncing against her cheek. "Nuh-uh." She sucked in a breath as she slid her body lower on his. "I'm all good."

Her small hand wrapped around his shaft and he twitched at the touch. "Penny ... ugh!" She was gripping him gently, as if she was unsure what to do. "That feels good." He rocked against her hand. "Fuuuck. Sweetheart."

"Will you make love to me again?" She asked, her cheeks tinting.

He nodded, then reached for the drawer in his night stand. Taking out the foil packet, her ripped the corner with his teeth.

"Let me," she said, taking the condom from him. She scooted down farther, planting herself on his thighs so she was looking at his cock, eyes wide. The face she made when she saw his erection would have been hilarious, except her hand stroking him made him growl instead of laugh.

"I don't want to hurt you again," he said as she rolled the rubber over his cock.

"I just have to get used to you. And make sure I'm ready." She reached down between her legs. The sight of her rubbing her sweet pussy made him grunt in approval. Her fingers slid over her clit and her slit, teasing herself until her breath came in little pants. He could smell her wetness, delicious and heady. Jesus, this was the hottest thing he'd ever seen. If he didn't get inside her right this moment—

"Damn, Penny you're going to kill me."

"Sorry!" She withdrew her hand.

"Don't be sorry," he growled. "But I need to be inside you. Now." He was surprised by the way he sounded. He usually wasn't so demanding in bed, but with Penny, he wanted to own her. Wanted to dominate her. Wanted to make her come over and over again until she couldn't think of anything but him.

She knelt over him, placing her knees on either side of his hips. He helped guide the tip of his cock against her slick cunt lips. Watching himself disappear into her was the hottest thing he'd ever seen. Penny moved her hips down, sinking down on him slowly. She was hot and tight and slick, and he never wanted to leave.

She let out a small whimper and threw her head back when he was fully seated inside her.

"You okay, sweetheart?"

She nodded, biting her lip as she stifled a moan. "Oh God. Ben. You feel so good inside me."

"*You* feel good." He pumped his hips up once and she cried out, clawing her hands down his hips.

She began to move, sliding his cock in and out of her. She was still so tight and hot, and he had to control himself or risk blowing his load too early. He grabbed onto the sheets and let her do her thing. She started slow at first, but as her breath quickened and her whimpers became louder, she upped her pace. Using her knees, she slid up and down his cock, her tight inner walls squeezing him tight.

"Hot damn." His eyes remained fixed on Penny as she rode him, her large tits bouncing up and down deliciously. He couldn't help himself and sat up so he could play with her breasts. Her eyes went wide with surprise and she lost her rhythm for a few seconds, but he encouraged her to keep going.

Penny braced herself by grabbing onto his shoulders, moaning as he leaned forward to take a puffy pink nipple between his lips. His teeth grazed the hard nub, and she let out a cry.

"Fuck!" He couldn't stop himself from coming as her pussy tightened around his cock. He thrust his hips up into her as he came, calling her name over and over again as he pulled her to him and tasted her delectable mouth. Her body spasmed, then she relaxed in his arms.

"Penny, you're incredible," he gasped as he collapsed onto his back, taking her with him so she lay on his chest again. He felt drained, but in a good way.

"Hmmm … you're pretty neat, too," she said with a sigh. "I guess we should get ready. You're already late for work, and I should get home."

She seemed almost sad as if she didn't want to be away from him. He felt the same way, but she was right. Ben rolled to his side, laying her down on the mattress as he slipped out of her. "Gimme a sec," he said as he kissed her forehead and got out of bed. He strode to the bathroom, quickly cleaned up, then walked back into the bedroom, pausing by the doorway to look at Penny.

She was laying on her side, eyes closed, and one arm under her head. His eyes roamed over the curves of her body, from her breasts down to the dip in her waist and the gently rounded stomach, to the thatch of neatly trimmed red curls between her thighs. His cock twitched at the sight of her naked body in his bed, and he wanted her again.

Penny opened her eyes and smiled at him. "Why are you looking at me like that?"

"Why not?" He approached the bed. "You're beautiful." He crawled over to her. "I'm sure the mines will be fine if I skip out today." Ben couldn't remember the last time he'd taken the day off.

"Are you sure?"

He lowered his head to kiss her square on the lips. "I'm sure."

CHAPTER 12

PENNY COULDN'T REMEMBER EVER BEING this happy in her life. Sure, there were maybe a few good memories in her childhood. Before this, the happiest moment in her life was when she left Greenville, but even that good memory was tied to bad ones. And there was Grams, of course. She had had some good times with her grandmother before she passed.

Okay, so it wasn't like her life had been miserable up to this point. But it was just so ... different. It was like all her life she'd been living in a haze, and now everything seemed so clear.

She smiled to herself, thinking of the last three days. After that first morning spent in bed, Ben took her back to Greenville so she could get ready for work, then they had dinner before her shift. Afterwards, he brought her back to his place where they spent the night making love again.

The memories made her cheeks hot. Although she had never been with anyone aside from Ben, she was pretty sure no normal human could have sex *that* much. She was pretty tired the next day, and Ben let her sleep in, leaving her a note to make herself at home. At lunch time he came home, and they didn't even get a chance to eat the meal she had prepared. She'll probably never think of his kitchen the same way again.

It was a good thing she had spare outfits at work because she hadn't gone home for three days. Last night was their busiest night, and she had spilled some beer on her jeans and really needed fresh clothes.

"Ben."

"Hmm …." He trailed kissed between her breasts.

"Ben!" She grabbed a handful of his hair before he could go lower.

"What?" he asked.

"I should go home."

"Huh?"

"I mean, I need clothes. And stuff. You know. Girl stuff." It was nice using his soaps, and he even got her a new toothbrush, but she just wanted to use her own things again.

"Okay, I'll take you home and you can pack a bag for the rest of the week."

Her mouth fell open, but before she could say anything else, a ringing interrupted them.

"Sorry," he said as he rolled over and reached for his phone. He turned around and spoke softly, nodding now and then. With a long sigh, he put down the phone.

"Everything okay?"

"Yeah," he said. "That was Jason. He says I have to go do wedding stuff tonight. We have security issues we have to work out at the castle, the mines, and the hotel."

Ben had told her the story of what happened at Matthew's wedding, how someone had snuck in a bomb that could have leveled Blackstone Castle. The thought that Ben could have been hurt or worse in that attack made tears burn in her throat. She didn't want that to happen at Jason and Christina's wedding. "You should go help."

He frowned. "I should, but I don't want to be away from you. Matthew asked Nathan, Luke, and me to take turns patrolling the area around the mines overnight. The Rangers will be there too, but Matthew wants someone he personally trusts to do it. I have to do the first shift tonight."

"I don't want to be away from you either, but everyone's safety is important." It seemed silly, but her stomach was knotting at the thought of not having him around, even for a night. "Go and help your family, Ben. They need you." She gave him a weak smile. "I'll be fine on my own, just for a night."

"It'll probably work out. I can take you home and you can get your car and a change of clothes."

"Yeah, it'll be fine," she said.

"Good. I'll pick you up for dinner as usual tomorrow." He crawled back into bed. "But first …."

"Watch it, butterfingers!"

"Sorry!" Penny apologized as the glass nearly slipped from her fingers. She steadied it just in time before it tumbled.

The guy she was serving shook his head. "Can't get good help these days," he said, shaking his head. His date laughed and nodded in agreement.

She took a deep breath. "Anything else, sir?"

He gave her a dismissive wave. "I'll call you when I need you."

"Of course." When she turned around and the guy couldn't see her, she grimaced. Why did that jerk have to sit in her section? He was the worst type of customer, snapping his fingers to get her attention and then making himself sound important to impress his date. She couldn't wait for him to leave.

Actually, she couldn't wait for tonight to be over. The moment she had walked into the employees' locker room, she knew there was something going on. Call it instinct or a woman's intuition. Whatever it was, it was clear the atmosphere had changed. Conversation between the other girls stopped, and the room went quiet. No one would look at her or even acknowledged her.

She had shrugged and thought it was just her imagination. Or maybe she was just too happy to pay attention. But, as the night progressed, that dread in the pit of her stomach grew.

One of the girls 'accidentally' picked up her drink orders and served them to another table. Someone in her section had given another server an order, but she 'forgot' to pass it on to her. And when it was time for her to take a break, everyone was 'too busy' to help her out, so she ended up skipping it.

As she walked back to the bar, she saw Olive leaning over the counter, whispering to Heather. The bartender's eyes clashed with hers, and as Penny gave her a smile, Heather looked away. Olive glanced at her, smirked, then sashayed off to her table. The pit in her stomach grew into the Grand Canyon.

"Hey, Heather," she greeted. "Can I have some soda water with ice please? I'm so thirsty."

Heather wouldn't look her in the eye. "Sorry, I'm out of soda water. You should go to the employee drinking fountain," she said in a flat voice before turning her back on Penny.

What was going on? "Okay then. Thanks anyway."

Heather didn't even acknowledge her.

Penny tried to ignore that sinking feeling in her heart. It wasn't her imagination. Something was going on.

She pushed the door that led to the back and walked toward the employee break room, her mind so preoccupied she didn't hear the footsteps behind her.

"Hey."

She jumped back in surprise, her hand going to her chest. "Oh." It was Mia. "I didn't hear you."

"You must have a lot on your mind," she observed.

"Yeah."

"Is it because of the other girls?"

Her face fell. "So they *are* ignoring me."

Mia's face scrunched up. "It's that bitch, Olive." She walked over to Penny and put a hand on her shoulder. "Listen, don't let them get you down. They're just jealous because they know about you and Ben."

"They know about us?"

She laughed. "He's been coming with you to the bar and taking you home for what—days now? I think it's pretty obvious."

"But why would the other girls be so mean to me? I didn't do anything ... he didn't date any of them before me, did he?" She never thought to ask Ben. The truth was, the thought of Ben with anyone else made her uncomfortable.

"Hmm, I don't think so, but," Mia leaned closer and lowered her voice, "I just heard Lana telling Olive that she saw you in Luke Lennox's car the other night. And then Olive told Heather the two of you must be having something on the side."

"No! That's not true!" Humiliation crept up her neck. "It's not! It's just Ben, I swear." She buried her face in her hands.

"I told you, Olive's a jealous bitch."

She looked up at Mia. "You believe me?"

"Those other girls, they're human, you know? I mean, they don't understand. You're Ben's mate, *right*?"

Was Mia asking or telling her? She paused, not knowing what to say. Was this something she was supposed to be keeping to herself? Was there some official ceremony or something?

"Well?"

"Y-y-yeah."

"So, you're his mate?"

She nodded.

"Oh. That's wonderful. Mates aren't as common as most people think, you know," Mia said. "But it's good that he's found you."

"I don't know what to do," Penny said in a deflated tone.

"Hmm. Well, why don't you ask me?"

"Really?"

"Yeah." She turned back to the door leading to the bar. "Oh shoot, they might be looking for us. But what do you say to lunch tomorrow? In town. You can ask me anything you want, and I'll help you. Maybe we can figure out a way to stop Olive from spreading those nasty rumors about you."

"Oh wow! That would be great!" For the first time that night, Penny thought things were looking up. "I can't thank you enough. You're too kind."

Mia gave her a grin that didn't quite reach her eyes. "Of course. Happy to help."

CHAPTER 13

Penny could hardly sleep last night. For one thing, she missed being wrapped up in Ben's arms. She couldn't even call him. He had explained that he'd be in bear form for most of the evening as he patrolled the mines, so he wouldn't be able to text or call her. So, she tossed and turned the whole night until she was so tired her eyelids felt heavy and she finally fell asleep.

She woke up late and knew she wouldn't make it in time for her lunch with Mia. There wasn't enough time to put on makeup or fix her hair, and though she knew she looked terrible, she didn't want Mia to think she was standing her up.

Penny breezed into the cafe where they set up to meet, craning her neck for a sign of Mia. But she was nowhere in sight, so Penny sat down at one of the empty tables. She was perusing the menu board when Mia walked in.

"Sorry about that," Mia said as she plonked herself down on the empty chair. "I slept in."

"I was a little late, too, so no worries."

They both got up to order at the counter, then brought their food back to the table.

"So, you're not from Blackstone?" Mia asked as she took a sip of her iced tea.

Penny shook her head. "I live over in Greenville." She gave Mia the short version of her story, about how her neighbor knew Tim and got her the job. "And you? Did you just move here?"

Mia laughed. "Oh, I just moved back." She took a bite of her sandwich. "I mean, I grew up here, but my parents had to … move away."

"You did? I mean, so you know some people here?"

Mia nodded. "But most of them probably don't remember me. That's okay, I wasn't one of the popular kids, you know?"

"Sure." Penny knew how that was. She had been the most *un*popular kid in school. "So, thanks for inviting me here."

"Oh, no problem. I hate those other bitches, you know?"

"Yeah, most of them were nice or just left me alone when I started."

"Until Olive spread those rumors about you."

Penny's shoulders slumped. "Yeah. I don't know why she's doing that."

"You know, I heard something about an incident in Greenville—"

"Oh no." Penny covered her face with her hands. *No, no, no.* Her throat burned with tears of humiliation. She bit her lip.

Mia pulled her hands away from her face. "If it's any consolation, I don't believe any of that."

"Really?" She wiped the tears from her eyes. "Thank you."

"Look, I'll do my best to stop those girls from talking about you, okay?"

"You will?"

"Of course!" Mia assured her.

"I can't thank you enough," Penny said. "I just don't want any trouble, you know? I just want to do my work."

"I understand." Mia looked over her shoulder and lowered her voice. "Now, there's something else I need to say. Uhm—" She stopped suddenly and shook her head. "Never mind. It's not my place."

"What is it?" Penny searched the other girl's face. There was a flash of apprehension in Mia's eyes. "Please, I owe you a lot. Just tell me."

Mia's eyes scanned the room, then she hunched her shoulders forward. "Well, it's about Ben. And … what he is."

"Huh? What do you mean? I know he's a bear shifter."

"Yeah, but … did you see him that night he shifted at The Den?"

Penny nodded.

"No bear is that big. Not even shifters."

"No?"

"No. Grizzlies, like Ben, are one of the biggest, but even they grow to ten feet max. I'm only six feet myself when I shift."

Penny shrugged. "He's big, so what?"

Mia lowered her lashes. "It's not just his size. The way he lost control like that? Shifters don't do that. I mean, not the ones in their right mind."

Penny grabbed the edge of the table, her fingers digging into the wood. "What are you saying?"

"Well, there have been rumors. I went to the same high school as him. I was two years younger."

"Did something happen?"

Mia paused, biting her lip. "It's none of my business really."

"No, please, tell me." Penny's heart was racing, but she wanted to know.

"Ben, he's different. So big and … dominant. There was this incident when he was at homecoming and he nearly mauled another student because he couldn't control his bear. Good thing the kid was a shifter and healed fast. If he had been human … he would have died instantly."

Penny couldn't control the gasp coming out of her mouth. "And then what happened?"

"No one knows for sure, but they probably paid off the family." Mia looked her straight in the eyes. "Penny, you should be careful. He's not what you think he is. He's … well, some say he's got a monster bear."

Penny stopped breathing. Fury was choking her. When the feeling passed, she expelled a breath. "You don't know what you're saying. Ben's no monster." Surely there was a good explanation. She stood up. "I think I should go."

"Penny, wait!" Mia grabbed her hand, her grip firm. "There's something else."

"I don't want to hear it." Penny tried to pull her hand away.

"He doesn't want you to know."

"Know what?" she asked.

"He and I—" The door slamming open cut Mia off. A group of women with young kids walked in, chatting as the children laughed and scrambled toward a group of tables in the corner.

Penny took the chance to pull her arm away from Mia and make a run for the door. She walked back to where she had parked her car, rubbing her arm. Mia's grip was so firm she left marks. What was she trying to say? Penny huffed. No, she didn't want to hear anything Mia had to say, not if she was going to talk about Ben that way.

It was still a couple of hours until her shift but too late to go home. She contemplated going to Ben's, but she didn't have a key. Plus, it sounded like he'd be tied up all day. After giving it some thought, she decided to just park at The Den and stay in her car until it was time to clock in.

By the end of her shift, Penny was exhausted. Not just physically but emotionally, too. She didn't know how much more she could take. Between the coldness and the snide looks, getting the wrong drinks from Heather, and no one helping her out, being at The Den was draining.

Then there was Mia. She'd avoided the other girl all night, though Mia tried to corner her several times. She didn't want to listen to what she had to say. If anything, she'd rather Mia ignore her, like the other girls did.

The work she once enjoyed was making her miserable, and she wasn't sure she could last much longer if they kept treating her like this. She didn't want to tell Tim; what could he do anyway? Tell the other girls they needed to be friends? Besides, she knew what happens when you tell someone in authority about people bullying you—you get labeled a tattletale and things get worse.

Penny didn't bother to say goodbye to anyone. She got changed, clocked out, and headed to the parking lot. As she was about to unlock her car, her phone began to ring. The name *BEN* flashed on the display. She wanted to weep in relief. "H-hello?"

"Penny." He sounded aggravated. "Where are you?"

"I'm just leaving work." She bit her lip. It was nice to hear his voice. "Should I drive over now?"

He let out a long sigh. "I'm sorry, Penny. Something came up."

"Is it bad?" She tried not to let the disappointment in her voice sound obvious.

"I can't explain now. But I'm not coming home."

"Oh." Her heart sank.

"I think you should sleep at your house tonight."

"Sure, that's no problem at all."

"Good." He paused, and she heard voices in the background. "Sorry, I gotta go. Lock your door, okay? Do you have Kate's number? Call her if you need anything."

"Sure."

The voices grew louder in the background. Was he at a party? "Penny, I—"

"You should go," she said, cutting him off.

"I'll see you tomorrow. I'll swing by The Den. I—"

"Bye," she whispered as she took the phone away from her ear and let the call drop. She leaned against the side of her car, her shoulders stooping. What was going on? Ben sounded agitated on the phone. Was he mad? And why couldn't he come tonight?

Penny sighed and climbed into her car. She needed to get some rest. No use getting worked up over this. She and Ben could talk in the morning. Putting the car into gear, she drove out of the parking lot.

Driving home from The Den was automatic at this point, and Penny found herself zoning out as she pulled onto the highway. Her thoughts kept straying back to Ben. They'd been apart for almost twenty-four hours now. Was he at some party? She didn't mind if he was, but she just wished he would tell her.

She was so distracted, she didn't notice the headlights

approaching from behind her. "Argh!" She covered her eyes with her hands as the glare blinded her when she tried to look in the rearview mirror. "Jerk." Some asshole in a jacked-up truck with his lights on, most likely.

Penny huffed and moved to the other lane, hoping they would pass. Instead, the vehicle switched lanes as well, and moved even closer behind her.

Her heart beat against her ribcage. "Don't panic," she told herself. She switched lanes again, and the truck followed her.

Annoyance was replaced by fear. It was strange because she'd never been scared driving alone back in Houston. But then again, no one had ever followed her.

She stepped on the gas, pulling as far ahead as she could and going over the speed limit by a few miles per hour. The truck sped up, too, and now her heartbeat was going a mile a minute. "Oh please, go away," she said aloud. Her exit was coming up, and they came up right behind her. Were there going to follow her all the way home? She racked her brain, trying to figure out what to do. An idea popped into her head, and she was suddenly thankful for whatever articles she had read that told her to do this.

Penny pulled off at the Greenville exit. The truck followed her. Instead of turning toward home, however, she went the opposite direction. Right into the parking lot of the Greenville P.D. The truck sped right past the police station and she let out a long sigh of relief. What the heck was that about? Was that guy drunk? Or was it just some asshole looking to get his jollies off?

She waited for a few minutes and then started her car again. She thought about giving Ben a call. Maybe the sound of his voice could help calm her and stop her hands from shaking.

She fished her phone out of her purse and dialed his number. It rang and then went to voicemail. Maybe he couldn't talk. He did ask her to call Kate if she needed anything. But then again, what would she tell her? It was silly now.

Penny straightened her shoulders. No, she should just go home. It was just some jerk driver being a Jerky McJerkface for the hell of it. She shouldn't bother anyone because she was being a silly worrywart.

CHAPTER 14

Ben turned off his phone and frowned. Penny had sounded strange. Was she okay? Maybe she was just tired.

His bear disagreed. It wanted him to drop everything now and be with her. And he wanted to, badly. This was the longest he'd been away from Penny and being without her made him antsy. But he couldn't. She would be safer tonight, away from Blackstone, especially after what he'd discovered earlier this morning.

"Everything okay, son?" James Walker asked as he came up behind him.

"Yeah, dad, it's all good." He slipped his phone back in his pocket. He was itching to tell his dad and mom about Penny being his mate. So many times he wanted to pick up the phone and let them know. But this was something he wanted to tell them face to face so he could see their reactions. Surely, they'd be ecstatic. And when Penny said she'd come to the wedding, he knew that was when he would introduce her to them. It would put less pressure on her since it was a big family event, rather than a dinner where she would be meeting just them. He couldn't wait. He told his cousins not to tell anyone about Penny yet, even his sister, and they agreed.

"Sorry we couldn't come earlier. Flight was delayed and then your mom wanted to make sure her dress was ready," James said. "I'm sure if she knew she'd be stuck at Blackstone Castle instead of coming to see you, she'd have put off that errand until tomorrow."

"It's fine, dad," he said. "Is everyone here?"

James nodded. "Yeah."

Father and son walked back into the trailer where Matthew, Jason, their father Hank, Luke, Nathan, and his father Clark were waiting. They were all gathered around the large table in the middle.

Since Matthew's wedding, Hank Lennox had told them about his plan to bring the Shifter Protection Agency to Blackstone. They were still working the details out with Aristotle Stavros, but everyone had agreed they would help and pitch in. While Stavros said it was unlikely that the anti-shifter group targeting Blackstone would attack again at the wedding, they weren't taking any chances, which is why it was necessary for them to patrol the main hot spots they might strike.

"So," Hank began. "Ben, tell us what you found."

Ben rubbed his hand down his face. "I was out with one of the Rangers last night, patrolling the mines. Everything was fine until about three a.m. We were in one of the older caves, the one from about three years ago, which we had shut down."

"What did you find?" Matthew asked.

"Fresh trace scents. Two or three different ones, but similar."

"Similar how?" Clark Caldwell asked.

"They were all bears, I'm pretty sure." Ben felt the muscles in his shoulders tense up, remembering how his own bear had raised its hackles when it scented the intruders. "There were some tracks, too."

"Shifter bears?" Jason asked.

"They must have been because that cave's pretty deep," James said. "I remember that one. No wild animal would just wander in there. We also boarded it up pretty well."

"What about humans?" Hank asked.

Ben knew what Hank was asking. There was a chance the humans who tried to blow up Matthew's wedding could be back, which is why they were doing the patrols in the first place. "No, Uncle Hank. No signs of humans."

"Nothing at the castle or hotel either," Matthew said. "We've got patrols 24/7."

"I don't get it. Bears? Are they working with the anti-shifters now?" Luke said.

"Could be related. Could be something else entirely," James said. "Or we may be worrying about nothing. Maybe it was a couple of teenagers fooling around."

"It doesn't feel right," Ben finished. His instincts were screaming at him. There was something wrong.

"All right," Hank said. "We'll have to be even more careful. All the women will be staying at the castle just in case, so it's easier to keep an eye on everyone."

"I hate to ask all of you to keep patrolling," Jason said. "This threat, it could be nothing."

"We're happy to help, bro," Nathan said. "Better safe than sorry. I don't want to end up in pieces if they manage to sneak another bomb in." He shook his head and laughed. "I hope this is the last wedding we'll have to be in."

Jason chuckled. "Me too. I'll be glad when all of this is over."

Ben looked at the men around him. Though Nathan's joke had broken some of the tension, it was obvious they were all still worried. He just hoped his instincts were wrong.

Ben wished he could go home and collapse in bed after spending the night roaming the woods. There was nothing he wanted more than to curl around Penny in his own bed. But there was work to be done at the mines. With Jason leaving for his honeymoon in a few days, they had to re-work the production schedule. Plus, there were a couple of things he had to take care of.

"Dr. Philipps, come in," he said to the older man who was standing by the doorway of his trailer office.

"Thanks for making time to see me today, Benjamin," Dr. Scott Philipps said.

"Of course, have a seat." He gestured to the chair in front of his desk. "What can I do for you?"

Dr. Philipps took off his glasses and put them in his shirt pocket. "Well, Benjamin, as you know, I've been with Lennox Corp for almost twenty years now."

"Has it been that long?" Dr. Philipps had been their chief geologist for as long as he could remember. He'd been a young boy when the doctor was hired. They never had such a position before, but his dad had recommended they get one to do research on blackstone and other minerals in the mountains. Dr. Philipps' work had been tremendously helpful, especially in searching for veins and determining more efficient ways of mining blackstone without harming the mountains.

"Time does go by quickly. Anyway, that's why I needed to talk to you."

"Oh." He could guess what this was about.

"Yes, it's time I retire. I love working here, but you know, I think I've earned some time off."

"Of course." Ben nodded in agreement. "You've been valuable to us, and I hate to see you go."

"Thank you for understanding. But I don't want to leave you in a lurch."

"I'm sure we'll find someone. Not as brilliant as you, but we can manage."

"I can stay on for a few more months, maybe until we need to move to another vein. But I do have a recommendation for a replacement," Dr. Philipps said. "As you know, I take summers off to teach back at my alma mater. I have a brilliant student who might be a fit for the job."

"Well, give me his resume, and we can see if he's a good fit."

"She, actually," Dr. Philipps said, "but I assure you, Dr. Robichaux is an utmost professional and highly sought-after in our field. And she's a shifter, if that makes any difference."

"I'm sure she's a fine candidate. Go ahead and send over her resume, and I'll look into scheduling an interview." They chatted for a few more minutes, until Dr. Philipps excused himself so he could contact his student.

Ben glanced at the clock. It was still early in the morning and, though he wanted to call Penny and hear her voice, he didn't want to disturb her if she was still sleeping.

"Boss! We need you in the smelting room."

He turned toward the door, where one of his guys was sticking his head in. "All right, I'm on it."

Ben spent the rest of the day working, his mind occupied

with all of the things he had to do. It was a good thing because he couldn't wait to leave. He tried to call Penny to see if she wanted to catch dinner, but she wasn't answering. Maybe she was driving or something, though it was still too early.

The long day was getting to him, so he thought he'd go home and nap or at least shower. Penny probably wouldn't appreciate his smell from the last twenty-four hours of patrolling and then working in the sweltering mines. He drove home, thinking of Penny and how me missed her. *Maybe I can convince her to clock out early,* he thought. He couldn't wait to see her.

He parked in front of his cabin, cutting off the engine, his mind still on Penny. However, as soon as he walked up to his front door, he smelled it. The same traces of a scent that had been in the caves.

Ben whipped around, scanning the tree line. There was no one there, but this was bad. His bear knew it, too. That unknown scent was making the bear uneasy. "Calm down," he said aloud. He had to keep his head.

He walked around his home, trying to find more traces, but he couldn't smell it anywhere else. That wasn't unusual. There had been a light drizzle this morning, so the rain would have washed away any trail.

"Fuck." He slammed his fist against the wall, leaving a dent in the middle of one of the logs. What the hell was going on?

He took his phone out of his pocket and dialed his dad's number.

"Ben?" James asked. "What's up?"

"They were here," he said, then explained what he had found.

"Shit. I'm coming now. I'll bring Luke or Nathan with me."

"Good," Ben said. Then he thought of Penny. It was a good

thing she wasn't in Blackstone but … if someone had been following him home, they might know about her. Why wasn't she answering her phone today? "Shit."

"Son?"

"Sorry, dad," he said. "I gotta go."

"What do you mean?"

"I have stuff to take care of." He had to make sure Penny was okay. His bear was angry now, snapping and growling at him. "I'll explain later, okay?" Maybe Penny should move into the castle too, just in case. This wasn't how he wanted to introduce Penny to his parents, but if she was in danger, he didn't have a choice. "I'll meet you back here, okay?" He hung up and ran to his car.

Ben made it to The Den in record time. By the looks of it, they had just started to get busy, with a couple of cars outside. He calmed himself and his bear as he walked through the door. He couldn't afford to have Tim seeing him agitated.

He scanned the room, looking for Penny. Did she not show up? A snarl escaped his throat.

"Ben?"

He pivoted around. It was that other waitress, the flirty one with the dark hair. The bear shifter. "Where's Penny?"

She frowned. "Sit down, there's something I have to tell you."

"Where is she? Is she hurt."

"Please. Sit down or Tim will kick you out," she said, nodding to Tim, who was standing in his usual spot behind the bar, keeping an eye on things. He wasn't looking their way yet, but Ben knew he'd notice if anything was off. "Fine." He sat down on the nearest chair.

"I'll pretend you ordered a beer and you drink it, okay?"

She put a hand on his arm, but he shrugged her away. "Just look … normal. And then we can talk."

"Fine," he said through gritted teeth.

She walked to the bar, chatted with the bartender and came back with a mug of beer. "Here," she said, sliding the mug over to him.

He stopped the mug with his hand. "Where's Penny?"

"Take a drink, big boy," she said. "Or Tim will—"

"Fine." He took a big gulp and wiped his mouth with the back of her hand. "Now where's Penny?"

"Shush!" She looked around. "Finish your beer and then meet me in the back as soon as you're done."

"Why won't you—"

"Just do it," she said. "If you care for Penny, you'll do this."

He wanted to shake her until she told him what was going on, but he couldn't risk it. "Fine."

"Mia," she said.

"Huh?"

"That's my name. Mia."

"Right." He looked away from her and took another sip of beer. She seemed to take the hint and left him alone, disappearing into the employees-only door.

Ben downed the beer and threw a couple of bills on the table. He got up, left through the front door, and made his way to the back entrance.

Something wasn't right. Why wasn't Penny here? And what did that other waitress know?

When he got to the back door, he saw Mia waiting for him. He strode over to her, his fists at his sides. "Tell me where she is."

"Oh, you know, she's around," Mia said, walking closer to

him. "But maybe I can keep you company until she gets here." She put a hand on his chest.

Ben snarled and caught her wrist. "Don't touch me, lady. Now what game are you playing?" He towered over her and walked her back until she was against the wall. "Don't make me ask again. Where. Is. Pen—" He let her wrist go and staggered back as he felt the ground tilt. *Huh? Was there an earthquake?*

Mia's mouth curled into a smirk. "Oh, are you okay, Ben?" she said in a mocking tone. "Did you get a little too much to drink?"

His vision began to blur at the edges. "You … the beer."

She tsked and shook her head. "Don't you know never to accept drinks from strangers? Then again, soon, I won't be a stranger."

There was something wrong in his system. His head was spinning, and he was losing his balance. He fought against it with all his might. "What did you do?" he roared as he lunged at her.

She easily evaded him, and he ended up slamming his shoulder against the wall. He spun around to face her.

"Don't worry Ben, the effects of bloodsbane are temporary, don't you know?"

Bloodsbane. The only thing that could bring a shifter down for long periods of time. They metabolized everything too quickly—alcohol, drugs, medications—but this was one thing that could take them down. *What was happening?*

Mia's eyes lit up. "Oh, and here's the part I've been waiting for." She raised a hand, which was now covered in black fur and tipped with razor sharp claws. He thought she was going to swipe at him, but instead, she ran a hand down her shirt, tearing the fabric into shreds. *What was she up to?*

"No, Ben, please don't!" she cried. "Stop! I told you, I don't want to do this anymore!"

"What ... the ..." His tongue felt thick, and he couldn't speak. He needed to get to the bottom of this. But when the sweet fruity scent hit his nose, he realized what was happening.

Penny was standing behind Mia, frozen to the spot. She must have been late, as she was still in street clothes, her purse slung over her shoulder and keys still in her hand. *Penny*, he wanted to scream. He raised a hand toward her.

"Oh Penny!" Mia cried, crocodile tears streaming down her cheeks. "I'm so sorry. So sorry. I tried to tell you."

Penny's eyes were wide, and her face grew pale. "I don't understand."

"I tried to tell you. But he threatened me. I swear Penny, he said ... he would hurt me if I tried to tell you."

"Tell me what?" Penny choked out.

"Ben and I ... we had a thing back in high school. My parents found out, and that's why we moved away. When I came back, we started things up again. We didn't tell anyone."

NO! I've never seen this woman before in my life! Ben was screaming in his head even though his mouth couldn't say it. His limbs felt heavy, and he had to brace himself against the wall to stay upright.

Penny turned to Ben. "Is this true?" Tears were gathering in her eyes, and her shoulders were shaking.

"He's drunk," Mia said. "He's always like this when he gets drunk. He can't control himself." Mia looked at Ben, a glint in her eye. "He's a monster."

Penny let out a cry. "Ben, please tell me this isn't true!"

Ben used all his strength to get up and say something, but

it was no use. It was like he was swimming in thick syrup. He tried to speak, but nothing came out.

"I think his silence speaks for itself," Mia said, grinning at Ben. When Penny turned to her, her face scrunched up and the tears started.

That two-face bitch! As soon as the bloodsbane wore off, he was going to tear Mia apart.

"I ...." Penny turned away from him, her shoulders shaking. "I can't ...." She began walking away, picking up her pace the farther she got.

NO!

Ben knew he had to fight the bloodsbane in his system. His bear was snapping its jaws and clawing at him from inside his skin. He knew there was only one way to break free of the drug's influence.

The bear let out an earth-shattering roar as it tore out of his human skin. Rage and fury filled its veins, and the bear bared its teeth at Mia.

Shock, then terror crossed Mia's features, and she let out a screech. Ben could feel the bear inside her cower in fear, unwilling to defend itself. His bear wanted to hurt that bitch for telling Penny all those lies.

Penny!

The massive grizzly swung its body away from Mia and charged in the direction Penny had run. She was in her car and slamming the door shut.

Ben pushed his bear's body, reaching out a massive paw to reach her before she could drive away. His eyes focused on Penny as she looked out the window and saw the look on her face. Horror. Panic. Fear.

The bear let out a pained roar as Ben pulled it back. It gave

Penny enough time to pull out of the parking spot and drive away from him.

Enough!

Claws tore down his face and chest, but he continued fighting his bear. Penny had been through enough. He wouldn't put her through more pain.

Mine!

No. Penny was lost to them now. The look on her face told him it was over. He really was a monster.

Ben struggled for control, and when he won out, he pushed his bear's body toward the woods. He had to get it away from Penny.

He should have told her the truth. But he knew now he had been selfish, wanting to keep her when there was no way this was going to end well. Not since that night at homecoming when his father told him the truth.

That damn Joshua Watson. He was the biggest jock in school but also the biggest jerk. He had taken Emma Reid to the homecoming dance as a joke. She'd been one of the plainest girls in school, a little on the plump side, and so shy. Of course, when they arrived at the dance, he started making fun of her, and all his friends joined in. Emma ran out of the gym in tears.

Ben had seen the whole thing, and he lost it. Emma was one of the nicest people in school and had never hurt anyone. He was only going to punch Joshua, but his bear came out. He nearly killed Joshua. If Joshua hadn't been a wolf shifter, he probably would have died.

It was pure chaos after that. The police were called, and his parents, of course. They smoothed things out with the school, the authorities, and the Watsons. But Ben had been confused. He'd never lost it like that, never felt so out of control.

Growing up, he had known he was different, not only because of his size, but also because of those uncontrollable urges inside him. And when he lost control, he knew something was wrong.

That was when James told him the truth.

"You know how Laura's not your birth mom, right?"

Ben had nodded. They had been truthful about that from the beginning. He and Laura had only known each other for six months when Ben came into their lives.

"Son, you've never asked about her. Your biological mother."

He had never needed to know. Laura was his mother, she raised him and that was that.

"Well, it's time you knew the truth. Sue, your mom ... she was a one-night stand, someone I had been with three years before I met Laura. But she was also a bear shifter like us. She was ... from the Bronson clan."

That revelation had shaken him to the core. The Bronsons were the Walkers' most hated enemy. They'd been warring for generations back in Morgan Valley. He had asked his father if he knew who Sue was when they met.

"No," he had said. "I didn't. But she knew who I was. Ben ... her father sent her to me. So she could get pregnant with you. She was going to bring you back to her clan, for God knows what reason. Maybe to use you as a pawn against the Walkers. She went back to them, pregnant with you. I didn't know and then she died. She left you with a friend and then you came to us."

That was the truth. He had looked up the Bronsons and had even gotten some info from his cousins. The Bronsons were a bunch of criminals and degenerates. While the Walker clan protected Morgan Valley, the Bronsons sought to take it over. They brought in drugs, guns, moonshine, and did all kinds of illegal activities, hoping to bring chaos. They hated the Walkers because of what they stood for and because they did everything in their power to stop them from dominating the Valley. The Bronsons did whatever the hell they wanted and didn't care about the consequences.

It was the Bronson blood in him that was making him uncontrollable. It made him a monster, just like everyone in that family.

Penny didn't need that in her life. She deserved better. And he knew this was the right thing to do. This line would end with him. There would be no mate and no cubs in his future.

CHAPTER 15

Penny didn't know what to do. There was no way she was going back to Blackstone. Ever. Not after what had happened.

Ben and Mia. She didn't want to believe it. Mia was a liar, calling Ben a monster. She didn't want to believe they'd been screwing around behind her back. But she'd seen it with her own eyes. Mia's shirt. Ben drunk off his ass and not even trying to defend himself. How could he when the evidence was there? And then he did turn into a monster and she knew it was all true. It had terrified her, seeing his bear come after her, and brought back memories of that night she had locked herself in the bathroom to get away from John.

Her brain was screaming that she'd been stupid to believe Ben. He'd just wanted to get into her pants, telling her that he was her mate. It was obvious none of that was true, not if he was seeing Mia on the side.

But her heart. Oh God, her heart. It hurt so bad. She knew why it was called heartbreak. She could feel her heart tearing itself apart. She crawled into a ball in bed, willing the pain to go away. She cried until she didn't have any tears left and then closed her eyes and let exhaustion take over.

The sun was high in the sky when she woke up. But it wasn't the sun that woke her; it was the knocking on the door. "Go away!" she shouted, throwing a pillow over her head. But the knocking didn't stop.

"Arrggghhh!" She sat up and rolled out of bed, stomping to the front door. She threw it open. "I said go—Dutchy?"

Dutchy was standing on the porch, a dress bag in one hand and a rolling suitcase in the other. "Penny! I've been calling you all morning! I have the dress ready, and I thought I'd come over to help you." Dutchy's brows knitted. "Are you okay?"

She had forgotten the wedding was today. "I'm ... not." It was embarrassing, really, breaking down in front of a near-stranger. But she couldn't help herself, and the tears just poured out of her.

"Oh my Lord!" Dutchy marched into her house, putting her things to the side. She put her arm around Penny as she sobbed. "There, there now," she soothed. "Penny, honey, what's the matter?"

"Oh Dutchy ... it's ... you don't have to ...."

"Oh shush! C'mon now, tell me what's wrong."

Penny hiccoughed, then took a breath. "I'm not going to the wedding."

"What? Why?"

"Because Ben ... we broke up. He ... he's not my mate." Though it embarrassed her to tell Dutchy what had happened, the whole pathetic story just spilled out of her mouth.

Dutchy placed a hand on her chest. "What? I can't believe he would do that!"

"I'm sorry you came all the way here for nothing," Penny said.

"What are you talking about?" Dutchy put her hands on her hips. "I didn't come here for nothing. You are *going* to that wedding."

"What? I just told you … Ben, he—"

"So, he's a cheating bastard!" Dutchy was shaking with anger. "And you know what the best revenge is, right?"

"What?"

"Showing up and looking so good that he regrets it."

"Dutchy, no! I don't want to go!" Penny just wanted to stay home in her pajamas and curl up in bed.

"No way, I won't allow it," Dutchy said.

"What are you going to do? Tie me up and dress me? Push me into the hotel in a cart?"

"C'mon, Penny! Live a little," Dutchy pleaded. "Besides, you need to do this for me! I need you to be there and wear my gown. Please? Pretty please? I'll dress you up and drive you. You don't have to stay long. Kate and Sybil will be there, right?"

And so will Ben. "I can't." But the forlorn look on Dutchy's face made her resolve falter. Dutchy really was kind to drive all the way here to lend her the dress. "Fine. But I'm only staying an hour. I'll talk you up nonstop during that time, but then I'm leaving." It was a big wedding, right? Surely she could avoid him for an hour.

"Oh, thank you, Penny! You won't regret this."

As she stood in line, waiting to get into the ballroom of the Blackstone Hotel, Penny dug her fingers into the soft tulle fabric of her skirt, wiping the perspiration that had built on her palms. She suddenly pulled away, not wanting to destroy the delicate fabric.

This was a bad idea. What if she'd been uninvited? Ben had said she didn't need a paper invitation. Christina had put her on the guest list because he would be at the private ceremony at Blackstone Castle, which was for family only, and they had planned to meet at the hotel.

As she neared the front of the line, her heart began to beat a mile a minute. It would be humiliating if she was told she wasn't on the list. She was all dressed up and everything. Dutchy had done a fine job with her makeup and hair. Penny felt like one of those glamorous Hollywood actresses from the 50s, with her hair in waves and her lips painted red.

When she reached the front and gave her name to the severe-looking woman in a tight-fitted suit, Penny held her breath. The woman looked down at her tablet, scrolled on the screen, then narrowed her eyes at Penny.

"You can go in, Ms. Bennet," Guest List Lady said, her expression unchanging. "Have a good time."

She breathed a sigh of relief and walked into the ballroom, carefully avoiding the gaze of the two very large and very intimidating men who were standing guard by the door.

The easy part was over. Now came the hard part. Mingling with guests and avoiding Ben at the same time. She wasn't sure how she was going to do that. She really only knew Kate, Sybil, and Christina. Catherine, she'd met only twice.

This was awkward. She came here for Dutchy, nothing more. Not even Dutchy's plan of 'making him drool and regret what he gave up.' She nodded while Dutchy was giving her tips on how to make Ben jealous, but all the while thinking of ways to avoid him.

As she walked around the ballroom, trying to make it seem like she was going somewhere, rather than stand awkwardly alone by herself, she was saved by the announcement over the PA system that the bride and groom had arrived.

Everyone hushed, and the lights dimmed. Music began to play, and the doors opened. Jason and Christina walked in, and everyone applauded.

"Oh." Penny put her hand over her mouth. What was it about weddings that made almost everyone cry? Christina looked beautiful, and Jason, well, he just looked so *happy*. He wasn't paying attention to anyone else in the room; in fact, it was like no one else existed but Christina. Penny brushed the tears forming in the corner of her eyes. She truly was happy for them, but there was that stabbing pain in her heart she couldn't ignore for long.

And then, as if on cue, Ben walked in behind them. He looked so tall and handsome in his tux, she nearly forgot to breathe. Had it only been a few hours since the incident? It felt like a million years ago. Only the fresh pain in her chest reminded her how it was just last night he had shattered her heart.

To make matters worse, he was strolling in with a beautiful blonde woman. She was gorgeous, tall, and elegant. She grinned at him, and he smiled back and drew her in for a side hug.

It was too much. Penny thought she'd be able to handle it, but seeing Ben with someone else was making her chest hurt again. Much more than it did last night. Ben was drunk last night, but today, he knew what he was doing.

She waited for the people to settle down, and, once the coast was clear, turned around and headed for the exit, going past Guest List Lady and the two guards.

"I swear I'm on the list. Can't you just let me in, please? I'm already dressed up."

"I'm sorry. I can't, miss," Guest List Lady said.

Penny froze. She knew that voice. Slowly, she pivoted on her heels. "Mia?"

Mia, dressed in a long red dress, turned around. "Penny?" Her eyes flashed with surprise for a moment, then a cool mask slipped on. "Leaving already?"

"Well, at least I was invited."

Mia's face twisted into an expression of hate. "I am invited. When you ran away, Ben asked me to be his date."

Penny knew that was a complete lie. Ben already had a date. "Really? Then how come you're not on the list?" Score one for Penny.

Mia's lips curled into a vicious smile. "Well, last night—"

"Penny!"

Her damn heart nearly leapt out of her chest at the sound of Ben's voice. He was standing by the entryway to the ballroom, disbelief on his face. "You came," he said. "You—" He stopped suddenly, and turned to Mia. "You," he snarled, then stalked toward her. "What are you doing here?"

"Ben!" Mia cried. "Ben, please!"

"You fucking liar!"

"No! Ben!" Mia cowered as Ben towered over her. He grabbed her by the shoulders and dragged her to Penny. "Tell the truth. Now."

"The truth?" Mia sneered. "That you've been sneaking around with me these past weeks?"

"Shut up! Tell her the truth! I've never seen you before, and you're not from Blackstone."

"Ben, you're scaring me," Mia said. "I am telling the truth."

Ben ran his fingers through his hair. "Penny, please, you

have to believe me. You're my mate! I swear I would never cheat on you."

Ben's words stunned her. Oh God, she wanted to believe him. She looked at Mia and then at Ben. Had she been wrong this whole time? She had to trust her instinct. Ben. It was screaming *Ben*. She opened her mouth to tell him but was interrupted by a shout from behind.

"What the hell is going on here?"

Kate was standing behind Guest List Lady, hands on her hips. Sybil was behind her, as was Ben's date.

"Kate!" Ben exclaimed. "Have you seen this woman before? Have any of you seen her? Do you know her?"

Kate shrugged. "Never seen her before."

Sybil shook her head. "Should we know her?"

The third woman walked closer and narrowed her eyes at Mia. Her nostrils flared, and she crossed her arms over her chest. "Who is she?"

Mia stood there, unmoving, her face a cold mask. She turned to Penny. "You should have stayed away, Penny. He's mine! He was meant to be mine!"

"Get her out of here," Ben barked to the two guards standing by the door. "Put her in the holding cell for a couple of hours." The men nodded and approached Mia. "Don't even think of shifting," Ben warned. "Those wolves are armed with special weapons to take you down. This entire hotel is surrounded by snipers, too."

"No!" Mia screeched as the two guards grabbed her by the arms. "Damn you Ben Walker! This was your last chance!" She let out a laugh as she was being dragged away. "You'll regret this! You and your mate are going to die!"

Penny felt a pit in her stomach slowly growing. Mia had been the one lying. All this time. She whirled around, covering her face with her hands. It was all clear now. Mia, manipulating her. Making her trust her. She'd bet everything she owned that Mia was the one spreading those rumors at The Den.

"What's going on? Ben, is she really your mate?" The tall blonde woman stared at Penny with a curious look on her face.

Oh no. Ben's date. Without a second thought, Penny picked up her skirts and ran.

"Penny!"

She ran as fast as she could, down the long hallway and into the lobby. She made it past the door to the outside, but she was no match for a shifter's speed.

"Penny. Stop." Ben was right in front of her, and she collided into his chest. He placed his hands on her shoulders to steady her. "Why did you run?"

Humiliation burned in her cheeks. "Ben, I should go."

"No!" he roared. "Why? I don't understand. You know she was lying. I was telling the truth, I swear. I would never cheat on you."

"That's why I ran!" she burst out suddenly. "Because you were telling the truth, and I didn't believe you!"

"What?"

She pulled away from him, wrapping her arms around herself. "Ben, I don't deserve you. I don't deserve any of this! I should have believed you last night, I'm sorry."

"Sweetheart," he said. "There's nothing to be sorry about. Last night wasn't your fault. Mia poisoned me. That's why I acted like I was drunk."

"She poisoned you?"

"Yeah. And she tried to make it look like ... well, I don't really know what she was up to."

Penny could guess. "She wanted you for herself."

"I guess." He frowned. "I just … please don't run."

"Ben, I should have trusted you. Don't you see? I don't deserve you."

"No!'" He grabbed her gently by the arm. "She was manipulating us. There's nothing to forgive, but if it makes you feel better, then I forgive you."

"I don't deserve it. I don't deserve you. What do you want with me, anyway? I'm just poor trash from the wrong side of town who—"

He cut her off with a kiss, pressing his lips to hers as he wrapped his steely arms around her. He kissed her until she was breathless and limp in his arms. "I won't have you talking like that. You're my mate, and I love you."

"You what?"

"I love you. You're mine and mine forever, if you'll have me." All of a sudden, his expression changed. The air shifted around them, and he let go of her. "Last night, I saw your face when I shifted. I know you were scared." He turned away, raking his fingers through his hair.

She reached out and touched his arm. "I wasn't scared of you. I was scared of my own demons. Seeing you like that brought up memories, but I know you would never hurt me." He remained silent as a stone. "Ben, talk to me."

He turned around slowly. "Mia was a liar, but she was telling the truth about one thing. I am a monster."

"I don't understand."

"Penny, I need to tell you the truth. And if you don't want to be with me, I'll respect your wishes."

"What truth? Please just tell me."

Ben's face was pure anguish. "It's the bad blood in me." Then, he told her the whole story. As he relayed it, Penny felt her heart breaking, imagining Ben as a young boy. Because she knew what it was like to have someone who was supposed to take care of you use you instead.

"Ben, I don't believe you're a monster."

"You've seen my bear twice. How could you not think that was a monster?"

"The first time I saw your bear, it was trying to protect me. How could I think of it as a monster?" She moved closer to him, placing a palm over his chest. "I know you, Ben. The real you. You told me you *are* your bear. Well, why can't the bear be *you*? You've got a good heart, so your bear can't be a monster."

He looked at her, his eyes like brilliant blue sapphires, the anguish on his face heartbreaking.

She lunged at him, wrapping her arms around his waist. "I love you, Ben. Both of you. All of you."

As he leaned down to kiss her, a warm feeling crept into her belly. It was faint, but it began to grow. Despite the chill in the air, she felt cozy, and not just because of Ben's body heat. Goose pimples broke out over her skin, and she shivered. A feeling washed over her, one she couldn't name, but it felt pleasant. For the first time in, maybe, ever, she felt calm. At peace. Whole.

"Penny?" Ben asked when he pulled away.

"Huh?"

"You felt that, right?"

"You did, too?"

He nodded. "The mating bond. We're really mated now."

"Oh my God." It was strange. She had always felt a pull toward Ben, but now it was like they were tied together. The warmth buzzing inside her felt incredible.

"I love you so much. You say you don't deserve me? It's me

who doesn't deserve you." He smiled at her. "How did I ever get so lucky?"

"Ben," she said with a sigh. "I love you, too. Oh no!" She pulled away.

"What's wrong?" he asked. "Did Mia say something else?"

"No. It's just that … what about your date?"

"My date?"

"Yeah, the blonde."

"The blo—" Ben laughed. "Amelia? My sister?"

"She's your sister?" *Huh.* She did kinda look like Ben, now that she thought about it. She was definitely tall enough to be related to him. "Oh poop, I feel silly now!"

"Don't be," he said. "I want you to meet everyone. Amelia. Mom and Dad. But," he pulled her back into his arms, "I think that can wait. I want to be alone with you for now, my mate. Let's go home."

"But the reception?"

"I've done my duty, and everyone will understand." He winced. "I'm sure Kate has told everyone that you're my mate by now. And they'll be looking for us, my mother especially. She's not going to be happy everyone else got to meet you first. We should go before she sends out a search party."

Penny was looking forward to meeting Ben's family, but it had been too long since they were alone together. "All right, let's go home."

CHAPTER 16

BEN DROVE BACK to his cabin as fast as he could without breaking any laws. He was still having a hard time believing this was real. That Penny really was his, and she loved him.

Last night, when he had gotten home after roaming the woods for hours, he collapsed on his front porch. He would have preferred to stay home and wallow in grief and shame tonight, but he knew Jason was counting on him to be at the wedding. So, he had gotten cleaned up and dressed. He had put on his best front because today was his cousin's and Christina's day and he wasn't going to ruin it.

And then he saw Penny at the reception, looking so beautiful. Hope had bloomed in him and he followed her when he saw her running. He couldn't help himself. And that bitch Mia. His bear growled. She was crazy. A stalker. He shook his head mentally. He didn't usually get that kind of women; it was mostly Jason or Nathan who attracted that type. He just hoped a few hours in the makeshift holding cell the wolves from Lykos had prepared would knock some sense into her.

Finally, they arrived at his home. He couldn't wait to get

her inside. He carried her up the stairs to the bedroom as she giggled adorably all the way. He laid her down on the bed, stripped her naked, and drank in the sight of her.

When he reached for the condom in the nightstand, she grabbed his hand and shook her head.

"Are you sure?" he asked. He couldn't bring himself to believe she would want his cubs, knowing about his bloodline.

"Yes. Ben, please, I want to feel all of you."

They made love slowly, enjoying the feel of each other. Somehow, it felt different this time. He couldn't describe it. Stronger. More intense. He felt like someone was plucking strings inside him, sending vibrating waves throughout his body. From the way she moved and cried, Penny must have felt it, too.

"Oh, Ben," Penny sighed as she fell on top of him.

He eased out of her and rolled her to his side. "I love you," he whispered. It felt good to say it. He wanted to say it over and over again and shout it to anyone who would listen.

"Hmm." She snuggled against him, burying her face in his side. "Ben, I—what's wrong."

He tensed. His bear's hackles rose. Something was wrong. His enhanced hearing detected sounds outside the house. Feet and paws shuffling.

"Get dressed," he said to her in a terse voice.

"What?"

"Please, Penny, just do as I say!" he barked. "Get dressed and stay in here. Lock the door."

His instincts were going haywire. He didn't know why, but there was a threat out there.

"Ben!" she called as he raced out the door. He didn't have time to explain but hoped Penny would obey.

As he reached the outside door, it suddenly went quiet. But he could sense their presence, whoever they were.

"Come out, come out, Ben Walker!" a voice called. "We know you're in there. We've got you surrounded."

He heard the revving of several engines, the cocking of firearms, and grunts and growls.

"We just want to talk. Now, we can do this the easy way or the hard way. The hard way probably involves a lot of pain for you and your mate."

"Fuck," he cursed. His bear was getting restless, sensing the danger they were in. He peeked out the window, so he could see if they were bluffing. They were not. There were two jacked-up trucks, several men with shotguns, and half a dozen full grown bears. They surrounded the front of his house.

"Don't even think of sneaking out the back; we've got that covered, too," the voice said, as if hearing his thoughts. "Just come out. Or we could force our way in."

Damn. He could maybe fight the bears, but not the men with shotguns before they pumped him full of bullets. Who were these guys, and what did they want?

He cracked the door open. "Fine! I'm coming out." He didn't really have a choice.

Ben pushed the door open and stepped outside, squaring his shoulders. He stood on the porch with his eyes staring straight ahead. "You all are trespassing. I suggest you leave now before I call the cops."

There were guffaws and laughs from the men holding the shotguns. The bears pawed at the earth and snarled at him.

"Trespassing? That's rich."

A figure stepped forward, leaving the line of men and bears. He was older but tall and built like a linebacker, with closed-cropped white hair and scars down his face. The scowl he wore cracked into a smile that didn't reach his eyes. With his physique, it was hard to guess his age, though he was probably much older than he looked. But the dominance he displayed was clear. He was the leader of this ragtag band.

The old man stalked closer until he was a few feet away from the porch. He crossed his arms over his massive chest. "Well now, it's nice to finally meet you face to face, boy."

"I'm not your boy," Ben roared.

He laughed. "I'll call you whatever the hell I want. The name's Amos Bronson, Alpha of the Bronson clan. And your grandfather."

Ben wanted to laugh at him but knew deep inside he was telling the truth. "What do you want?"

"What do I want?" Amos roared. "I want what's owed to me."

Ben tensed. "I don't have whatever it is you think is yours."

"Don't be stupid, boy. I want *you*." Amos craned his neck up at him. "Since you're not denying I am your grandfather, let me bring you up to speed. I sent my eldest daughter, Sue, to seduce your daddy."

"So, you're a bastard who offered up his own daughter to his enemy."

"Wanna know why?" Amos didn't wait for him to answer. "Why do you think your bear is so massive? And your daddy's? It's because your line is infused with dragon's blood." He spat. "I knew I needed that in my clan, too. You were going to be the start of a new generation of Bronson bears who would be the meanest and most dominant in the world. And the fact that your daddy's a Walker was icing on the cake. It would have been the biggest slap in the face to that clan."

"Well, my father got to me first," Ben said. "Too bad for you."

"It was your bitch mother!" Amos said, the rage barely contained in his voice. "She ruined everything when she ran away with you as soon as you were born. It took us years, but we got her. Too bad she had already tucked you away by that time."

"You lost, get over it. Why did you come here?"

Amos' voice grew cold. "You were supposed to fall for the same trick your daddy did, and I was going to make sure your cub didn't get away. But my granddaughter is too stupid to seal the deal." Amos nodded to a shadow in the corner, and someone stepped forward. Someone familiar.

"Gramps, I told you," Mia said in a petulant voice. "I almost had him! If they had taken care of his whore mate, then I could have given you what you wanted."

"Yeah, well, maybe you're not a good as you think you are," someone standing on the far right said.

Ben's head whipped toward the familiar voice. It was Tyler, the man who had interviewed at the mines a couple of weeks back. Beside him was the other man, the simple one, Rick.

"Howdy, cousin," Tyler said with a grin. "Never did hear that callback from your HR. But that's okay, we wasn't really there for a job, right Rick?" Rick nodded. "We was scoping out the place. We've been going in and out at night for the last couple of days. Not that we could find anything useful."

So it was them. They were the ones who were in the abandoned cave. That means they were also the ones who had prowled around his cabin.

"We've been keeping tabs on you, boy," Amos said. "Ever since we found out your daddy got you. Been watching your every move since you were a boy. We know everything. About homecoming, about you going to Colorado State, and of course, your sweet little mate."

"Pretty one, ain't she?" Tyler leered. "Too bad she scared so easy."

"What the fuck are you saying? You've been following her?" Rage was building inside him.

"We was gonna get rid of her, but she was too smart, that one," Tyler said.

"Shut up, all of you!" Amos boomed. "No more talking. I'm here to finish this, since my own grandchildren are too stupid to get things done." Tyler and Mia tried to protest, but he silenced them with one hand. "Let me lay out what's going to happen," Amos said, turning to Ben. "You're going to join us, boy. Leave Blackstone and come with us."

"Why the hell would I do that?"

Amos's lips thinned into a smile. "Because I know you've got your pretty little mate tucked in there." He leaned his head back and took a sniff. "Hmm ... I can smell her from here. She smells sweet."

Ben gritted his teeth. "You'd have to go through me first."

"I could, and I will," Amos said. "But then what would happen to her when you're not here to protect her? You know there are things worse than death."

"You bastard!" His bear roared deep inside him, and a growl tore from his throat. "You lay a hand on her—"

"Shut up and listen to your grandfather, boy!" Amos raised a hand and several barrels pointed toward Ben. "I know dragon scales are bullet proof, but what about bears with dragon blood? Care to test it?"

Ben froze. His bear wanted to fight, but he willed it to stay calm. There were too many of them, and those guns would slow him down.

"Ready to join us boy?" Amos sneered. "As long as you do as I say, she'll be safe."

Ben gritted his teeth, and his hands curled into fists at his sides. "My father, my cousins, and Hank Lennox will come after you."

"When? Tomorrow when they're done partying? I'll have you and Penny in my territory by morning. And you'll tell them you're joining me willingly if you want to keep your precious Penny safe."

"Why are you doing this? You've got an entire clan under you? Why me?"

For a moment, Ben saw something in the old man's eyes he hadn't yet seen. A flash of fear. It was quickly replaced by a hard glint. "Don't you know what's coming boy? They're coming for *us*. They want war. And we need every strong bear to fight them off and keep our own safe."

"Who? Who are you talking about?"

"Them. The—" Amos eyes grew wide as an ear-splitting screech broke through the air. The trees shook as strong gusts of wind blew over them. Overhead, something very large and gold flew by.

Uncle Hank, Ben thought in relief.

"Fuck!" Amos cursed as he grabbed Mia by the arm and dragged her to him. "You said those fuckers were still busy at their party!"

"They were when I got away from those wolves!" Mia cried. "I swear, Gramps, they were all guzzling champagne like there was no tomorrow!"

"You stupid bitch!" He threw her down on the dirt. "Goddammit!"

Another whoosh of wind. A second dragon flew above them. Ben heard the long huff of breath and knew what was coming. He covered his eyes as the fire rained down. The smell of burning fur and flesh filled the air, along with the sounds of screams and growls. He heard a lion roar and several wolves howl from deep in the winds.

"NO!" Amos screamed. "You'll pay for this, boy!" An enormous dark brown grizzly tore out from Amos' skin. It raised its paws in the air and then headed straight for him.

It took only a split second for his own bear to rip out of him. He was much bigger than Amos, of course, and younger, but he wasn't going to underestimate the old man. Amos was probably nearing 70, but he was a shifter and in good condition. Plus, he had nothing to lose now.

The two bears clashed in a flurry of teeth and claws. Amos managed to get him in his side, his claws leaving a trail of blood down Ben's rib cage. Ben roared in anger, and though he wanted the old man to suffer for everything he did and what he was planning to do to Penny, he just wanted this to be over even more. He used his paws to bring Amos down to the ground and push his head into the dirt, then sank his teeth into the other bear's neck. As soon as blood gushed into his mouth, he let go of Amos' neck and staggered back.

Ben pushed his bear back inside him. It had done enough, and he needed to take his body back. As he lay dying, Amos, too, began to transform back into his human form.

"B-b-boy," he called in a weakening voice. "They're coming. They're …." His eyes rolled back as the life slowly seeped out of him.

A chill blasted across his arms, causing the hair to stand straight up. What did Amos mean? Who was coming for them?

"Ben!"

He whipped around. Penny was standing by the door,

barefoot and dressed in his shirt. Her face was pale and her eyes wide. When she tried to look down, he quickly ran to her, putting himself between her and Amos' body.

"No, don't look."

"Oh, Ben!" She clung to him, wrapping her arms around his torso. "I was so worried!"

"It's done," he said, rubbing his hand down her back. "No one will ever hurt you."

"Ben!"

Nathan jogged up behind them, barely transformed back as grey fur receded into his body. "You all right?"

"Yeah, we're good." Ben looked around him. Most of the members of the Bronson clan were incinerated by Matthew's dragon fire. He was sure a couple escaped, including his cousins. He shuddered at the thought. Amos was a mean bastard, and he did his best to make his grandkids just like him. He wondered what would have happened to him if his mother hadn't run away with him. Would he have been like them? He turned to Nathan. "How did you know to come?"

"Penny called Kate," Nathan said. "And Kate told us. Jason and Christina had just left for their honeymoon, and things were winding down."

"You called for help?"

Penny nodded. "I knew something was wrong. I came down, and when I heard who that … that man was, I ran back upstairs and called Kate."

He took her into his arms. "My mate is one smart cookie."

They broke apart and joined Nathan and everyone else as they surveyed the damage. Uncle Hank and Matthew had flown his dad, Luke, Nathan, and Uncle Clark, since that was the fastest way up the mountain to Ben's cabin. They had also called the Rangers for backup. As Matthew's fire rained down, the others had flanked the rear to catch those who got away. Meanwhile, Uncle Hank had taken care of the bears guarding the back.

"There's no one left," Matthew said. "The Rangers caught the last three."

"My cousins," Ben said, the words leaving a bitter taste in his mouth.

"What should we do with them?"

"Lock them up. Throw away the key. I don't care." Ben squeezed Penny closer to him. "I just never want to see them ever again."

A car pulled into his driveway, one he recognized as Sybil's. The door flew open, and Laura Walker came running out.

"Ben!" she cried as she threw herself against him. Penny stepped away quietly, giving his mother room. "Oh my God, I thought we were going to lose you." Laura was shaking as he embraced her.

"I'm here, Mom, I'm here."

Laura didn't let go for a full minute until James came and gently pried her away. "I'm sorry, son," he began. "This never should have happened."

"It's not your fault, Dad," Ben said, then told them everything about his mother and Amos' plan. Both of them had stunned looks on their faces by the time he finished. "I knew it. I did come from bad blood."

"No, honey, don't say that." Laura came forward and touched Ben's cheek. "I always wondered why she would just give you up. Then I became your mother, and then Amelia came, and I understood what it was like to have this person who you love more than anything in the world and you'd do anything to protect."

"She must have loved you so much," Penny added. "That's not bad blood, Ben. That's good. Good through and through, just like you."

Ben's throat burned with tears. At what he had lost even though he had been too young to understand. And the mother who must have loved him enough to give her life, so he didn't have to suffer a childhood that surely would have turned him into a real monster.

"We had her buried in the cemetery in Verona Mills," James said in a somber tone. "Laura makes sure she has fresh flowers every year on the anniversary of her death."

"I'll start visiting," Ben said.

Laura smiled, even as tears streamed down her cheeks. "This is some night, isn't it? But I think there's something more important you have to do."

Ben frowned. "What?"

"Introduce us to your mate," Laura said as she looked at Penny, her smile growing even wider.

"Oh. Yeah." Ben put an arm around Penny and pulled her forward. "Mom, Dad, I'd like you to meet Penny Bennet." He looked down at Penny, his chest bursting with so much pride he could barely breathe. "My mate."

EPILOGUE

Two months later ...

Penny picked up the heavy basket with both arms, letting out an un-ladylike grunt as she lifted it out from the backseat of her car and placed it on the ground. *Maybe I shouldn't have packed so much food.* But she wanted to surprise Ben. Though he'd probably be surprised enough once he saw the gift waiting at the bottom of the picnic basket.

"Mrs. Walker, can I give you a hand?"

It took Penny a few seconds to respond. She was still getting used to being called 'Mrs. Walker' by the employees at the mines. She turned around. "Oh thank you …."

"Mike, ma'am," the young man said as he picked up the basket with ease. "Where would you like me to take this?"

"Let's go over there." She pointed to the clearing behind a row of trees. She and Ben often had lunch there; in fact, that was the spot where Ben had asked her to marry him. He didn't even wait a week after they were mated to ask. She said yes, of course, and they were married shortly after.

"Right here's fine," she said to Mike as they reached the shady spot under some trees. "Thank you so much."

"Welcome, Mrs. Walker. Anything else I can do?"

"Yes, if you could call my husband, that would be great."

"Will do." Mike gave her a two-finger salute as he walked back toward the mines.

My husband, Penny said to herself as she began to unload the picnic basket. The words still felt alien to her ears, but her heart would always swell at the sound of it. And to think, their wedding had almost been a disaster, thanks to none other than her own mother.

Penny had left Greenville to live with Ben right after the night his grandfather's clan had attacked them. Without their Alpha, what remained of the clan had scattered in the wind, but Ben wasn't taking any chances. They sold her trailer and paid off some of her dad's medicals bills, and she moved in with Ben. She was at the bank, signing the final papers of the sale when news of the scandal broke.

Coach John Stevens was caught having an affair with a sixteen-year-old student at Greenville High. He claims it was consensual, but the girl's parents had pressed charges anyway. He was immediately fired, of course, and was now awaiting his trial at the county jail.

Penny wasn't sure how to feel about it; in fact, she buried it deep inside, not wanting the old memories dredged up when the happiest day of her life was approaching. She had told Ben about it, and while he respected her need for privacy, he said he would be there whenever she was ready to talk and support her in whatever she wanted to do.

She really was ready to let go. But then, her mother showed up on her wedding day. At first, she thought her mother was ready to apologize for what had happened years ago, but it turned out, she thought it was her right to be there as the mother of the bride. Eleanor didn't even want to talk about John. And so, without a second thought, Penny had her thrown out.

Maybe she should have felt some remorse over what she had done and some vindication over what had happened to John. Some closure, maybe. But she felt *nothing*. It scared her, but later, Ben told her that sometimes when something is done, it's just done. Only you get to choose when something is over and that should be closure enough. And perhaps it was a good thing that happened on the day she was starting a new life. Speaking of which—

"What's this?"

She turned around to find Ben standing behind her, a big smile on his face. "Surprise!" she said and moved closer to him. He immediately took her into his arms, lifted her up, and kissed her on the mouth. She melted against him, her knees weakening. Even after all this time, it still felt like that first time they kissed.

"It's not my birthday or anything," Ben said, his brows knitting together. "What's the occasion?"

"Oh no occasion," she said with a laugh. She hoped Ben didn't hear the nervousness in her voice.

She sat down on the blanket she had laid out and motioned for him to sit beside her. Then, she opened the basket and started handing him the various containers inside, and they began to eat the feast she had prepared. Mac and cheese, meatloaf, mashed potatoes, buttered vegetables—all of Ben's favorites that Laura had taught her how to cook. They chatted as they ate, and Ben polished off most of the large meal.

"I'm stuffed," he said as he put down his plate.

"Finally?" she teased.

He laughed. "Yeah. But maybe I could go for some dessert." He grabbed her by the waist and pulled her onto his lap, making her straddle him. He pressed his mouth to hers in a long, lingering kiss. "Hmmm," he said as he pulled away. "Sweetest thing in the world."

"Ben …," she whispered, then suddenly remembered why she was here. She rolled off him, then smoothed her skirt. "Um, there's actually one more thing … could you look inside the basket, please?"

"Oh, did you really bring dessert? What is it?"

"Just go look."

Ben reached for the basket and placed it on his lap. Opening the top, he reached around inside, his face lighting up when he found the gift she had left there. He took out a plain cardboard box. He shook it, shrugged, and then opened the container.

Penny's heart began to speed up like a locomotive as she watched Ben reach inside and take out the one item she had placed in there.

His face was a mask of confusion as he took out the tiny shoe from the box. He stared at it for a second, then slowly turned to her. "Penny … are you …."

"Yes."

He let out a loud whoop and then picked her up in his arms and swung her around. "We're having a cub!" he shouted. "I—Oh no!" He quickly put her down and then placed a hand over her belly. "Are you okay? Did I hurt you? Did I hurt the baby?"

Penny laughed. "No, no, not all! He or she is still very tiny."

His face was beaming with pride. "I don't think I could be happier than this moment. Who else knows?"

"No one. Well, except Kate. Because you know—"

"Kate is nosy," Ben finished with a laugh. "We'll tell Mom and Dad over dinner this week."

"I can't wait."

They packed up the picnic, and Ben put the tiny shoe in his pocket, promising he'd carry it from now until the baby was born. As they walked back toward the mines, an unfamiliar car pulled in front of the office trailers. The driver's side door opened, and a figure stepped out. It was a woman dressed in a white suit and stiletto heels and holding a leather briefcase.

"May I help you?" Ben said as the woman approached them.

The woman smoothed a hand over her midnight-black hair tucked into a neat bun. Light blue eyes tinged with a dark blue outer rim stared back at them. "Good afternoon," she said, her voice low and husky. "I'm looking for Dr. Scott Philipps or a Mr. Benjamin Walker."

"Dr. Philipps is still in the mines, but I'm Ben Walker."

"Oh excellent," she said, holding her hand out. "I'm Dr. Violet Robichaux."

Ben shook it. "Dr. Robichaux. You're coming in for an interview today."

"That's right."

"We can do that now. Oh, this is my wife, Penny," Ben said.

"How do you do, Mrs. Walker?" Dr. Robichaux greeted in a formal tone, her voice posh and refined.

Penny couldn't help but stare. Violet Robichaux was beautiful in an unusual way—heart-shaped face, alabaster skin, and those strange eyes. They were almost hypnotic. "Um, I'm great. Nice to meet you."

"Let's go this way," Ben said, motioning to his trailer office. The three of them started to walk over but stopped when they heard a loud voice from behind.

"Ben! Goddammit Ben, wait up!" Nathan called as he ran up toward them. "That fucker Jenkins left the fucking grinding machine on again during his break! I told him I was going to tear him limb from limb and piss on whatever was left if he ever—" He stopped short, skidding on the gravel right before he ran into Dr. Robichaux. His body tensed, and a growl emanated from his chest.

Dr. Robichaux stared at him and her nostrils flared. "Oh," she said in a breathy voice.

"Oh?" Nathan echoed, his eyes glassy.

"Oh. No." She shook her head. "This simply won't do."

"Huh?"

"No, this won't do at all." She straightened her shoulders. "I appreciate you and your wolf's interest, but I'm afraid I can't have a mate at this time. So, thank you, and I wish you well."

Nathan continued to stare at her but didn't move an inch.

Dr. Robichaux turned to Ben. "Mr. Walker, could we get on with the interview, please? It was a long flight, and I'd really like to go back to my hotel and rest."

Ben didn't answer her right away as he was giving Nathan a strange look. Penny nudged him in the side. "What? Oh yeah. Penny, sweetheart, could you show Dr. Robichaux to my office? I need to talk to Nathan."

"Of course," Penny said and led the other woman away. She glanced back and saw Ben talking to Nathan, who shrugged and walked away, kicking a rock in his path and shoving his hands into his pockets.

"Go right inside," Penny said to Dr. Robichaux. "I'm heading out. It was nice to meet you."

"Lovely to meet you as well," she said before stepping into the trailer. As the door closed behind her, Ben came jogging up. "What was that about?" she asked. "Did I really hear her say mate? What did Nate say?"

Ben sighed. "I'll tell you later," he said, drawing her close and placing his chin on her head.

Perhaps it was their mate bond, but it was like she could feel what he was feeling, the joy in his soul when he put a hand over her belly. "I love you," she said warmly.

"I love you, too." He was smiling at her, but there was an uncertain look behind his eyes.

Penny sensed something else in him. "What's wrong, Ben? Are you regretting this?"

"What? No! Don't ever think I'm anything but ecstatic that you're having my baby. It's just … the stakes seem higher now. I have so much more to lose."

She put her hands on her hips. "Ben, you're not going to lose us. I know you're going to keep our baby safe. And as long as we're here in Blackstone, we have family to protect us."

"You're absolutely right," he said, giving her a kiss on the nose. "I promise you, you and our cubs will be safe forever."

Penny's eyes shone with tears because she knew deep in her heart Ben would keep that promise. She would always feel safe and loved in his arms. Grabbing his hand, she placed it over her belly. "I *know* you will."

The End

Thanks for reading!

Want to read a **BONUS SHORT STORY** from this book? <u>Sign up for my newsletter by logging onto:</u>
http://aliciamontgomeryauthor.com/mailing-list/

You'll get access to ALL the bonus materials from all my books, two FREE contemporary novels and my **FREE** novella **The Last Blackstone Dragon,** featuring the love story of Matthew's parents, Hank and Riva.

PREVIEW: THE BLACKSTONE WOLF

Nathan threw the wrench he was clenching in his hand, the metal making a loud clanging sound that echoed through the cave. He wiped a greasy palm down his pants. He was not having a good morning. First, one of their smelting machines had broken down and it took hours to get it back up. Then, he found out they were going to have to relocate the next site as it had not contained as much blackstone as they thought. Months of planning down the drain. They would have to work double-time since they were now behind in their production schedule. And now *this*.

"And if you leave this machine on again while you take your break, I'm gonna to tear you limb from limb and piss on what's left!" Nathan roared.

"Y-y-yes sir, Mr. Caldwell," Bryce Jenkins said as he cowered.

The smell of fear from other man was unmistakable, and his fox was crouching in terror. But Nathan didn't give a shit. He hated it when people disrespected machines, especially the ones under his care. Carelessness could cause accidents, not to mention lives. And Lennox Corp., who owned the Blackstone mines, always put the safety of their people above everything else which meant *he* was the one responsible for making sure the equipment ran smoothly and didn't kill anyone.

"Get out!" he snarled.

"S-s-sir?" Bryce stuttered. "Am I fired?"

"No!" He couldn't unilaterally make that decision of course; besides, he knew Bryce would probably never do it again. The younger man was inexperienced, not stupid. "Just get out of my face for now."

"Y-y-yes sir!" Bryce backed up slowly. When he'd put enough distance between them, he turned and scampered away.

"Fuck my life," he said aloud. He gritted his teeth. Someone getting hurt would be the perfect icing for this shit cake of a day. He had to talk to Ben.

Nathan marched out of the cave, deciding to check if Ben was in his office. He immediately spotted Ben and Penny, hand-in-hand, heading to the group of trailers around the main parking lot. He jogged toward them, picking up his pace.

"Ben! Goddamnit Ben, wait up!" He ran faster. "That fucker Jenkins left the fucking grinding machine on again during his break! I told him I was going to tear him limb from limb and piss on whatever was left if he ever—"

Nathan didn't notice the third person with them until he was much closer. Gravel skidded around his work boots as he tried to prevent his momentum from crashing into her, causing him to stop centimeters away.

A sweet scent, like golden honey with an underlying tinge of fur, assaulted his nostrils. He didn't mind; after all, he had a sweet tooth. He stared at the person—no, the woman—in front of him. A gorgeous heart-shaped face. Smooth skin that would surely be soft to touch. Thick, dark hair in a neat bun he longed to set free. Light blue eyes tinged with a darker color along the edges. And they were staring right back at him.

Mine, his wolf growled.

And he felt her animal—whatever it was—roar it right back.

The woman's nostrils flared and her pupils dilated. His spine stiffened, and a growl escaped from his throat.

Shit. This was her. His *mate.*

His brain started turning after what seemed like an eternity. Mate? Him? No, that couldn't be right. He didn't want a mate. He was not ready to settle down yet.

"Oh."

"Oh?" *Was she so stunned that she was speechless?*

"Oh. No." She shook her head. "This simply won't do." Her voice was low and husky with a rich timbre that washed over him like a lover's caress.

"Huh?"

"No, this won't do at all." She gave him a quick once-over, then straightened her shoulders. "I appreciate you and your wolf's interest, but I'm afraid I can't have a mate at this time. So, thank you, and I wish you well."

What. The. Ever. Living. Fuck.

The woman turned to Ben. "Mr. Walker, could we get on with the interview, please? It was a long flight, and I'd really like to go back to my hotel and rest."

Ben was looking at Nathan, his eyes wide. Penny had to elbow him to get his attention. "What? Oh yeah. Penny, sweetheart, could you show Dr. Robichaux to my office? I need to talk to Nathan."

"Of course," Penny said with a nod, and the two women began to walk in the direction of Ben's office.

"Nathan?" Ben began, his voice unsure. "You okay man? Is she your—"

"No way," Nathan said.

"Look, man, I know how it feels when you think your mate is rejecting you, but—"

"You heard her. She doesn't want a mate."

"So? If she's yours—"

"Newsflash Ben: I don't want her either. You think I want a mate?" He let out a laugh, not caring if it sounded forced. "I'm drowning in so much pussy, especially now that you and Jason are off the market. I can have any girl I want. Why would I give that up for some chick?"

"Nathan, you can't stop fate—"

"Don't, Ben. Just don't." He turned around, kicking a rock in his path and shoving his hands into his pockets as he walked away.

Mate? Fuck that. Who the hell needed a mate when freedom was much sweeter?

Besides, she wasn't *that* pretty. She seemed cold and unfeeling. And what was she wearing? She looked out of place wearing a white suit and stiletto heels in the mountains. What kind of interview was she doing with Ben?

His wolf snarled in jealousy thinking of her and Ben alone in his office. *Stupid wolf.* "For fuck's sake, Ben would cut his own balls off before he cheated on Penny," he told his animal.

"Mr. Caldwell, sir!"

He stopped in his tracks and turned around. It was Morris, the smelting room supervisor. Based on the man's face, he wasn't bearing good news.

"What is it?"

"You need to come see this, sir."

Nathan groaned inwardly. He pushed aside thoughts of honey and fur and light blue eyes. "Fine. Show me what's wrong *now*."

Violet Robichaux was sitting on the chair in front of the large oak desk waiting patiently for Benjamin Walker to come inside to start the interview.

Mine, her tiger hissed. *Mine.*

So that foul-mouthed man—wolf—was supposedly her mate?

Those really existed?

Violet didn't have any shifter peers in the New Orleans neighborhood where she grew up. She had a *normal* upbringing, which her parents had strived to give her. They weren't mates either; they had explained they chose each other because their personalities were suitable. They had similar goals, and it didn't hurt that they were both shifters *and* scientists. Her father was a chemist and her mother was a botanist. Of course, had one of them been a geneticist, perhaps they wouldn't have thought they were so compatible. Recessive genes, after all, had higher chances of mutations, which her own animal certainly was.

Mine, it insisted, interrupting her reverie.

"Oh hush," she said aloud. "I *told* you this can't happen. Not now."

It growled unhappily, but she pushed it away deep inside her so she didn't have to listen to it whine. She wouldn't have gotten this far in her career if she gave in to her animal's demands all the time. Science required discipline and dedication. Her parents, who were also at the forefront of their own fields, taught her that. It was hard enough for a woman in STEM to get ahead, but a shifter, too? She'd learned to hide that part of her over the years by controlling her inner animal.

And now it seemed to want to break free. All for a wolf. The irony.

She supposed he was attractive in that conventional bad boy kind of way, but he wasn't her usual type. Like most shifters he was tall and built like a bodybuilder, though he looked like someone who liked to work outdoors and with his hands. The way his white shirt clung to his broad shoulders and chest was practically obscene. And his dark blond hair was a tad too long, although she wondered what they would feel like between her fingers—

The sound of someone clearing their throat jolted her out of her thoughts. "Dr. Robichaux?" Ben Walker said as he walked through the door. "Sorry to keep you waiting. I had to see my wife off."

"Not a problem."

He sat on the worn leather chair behind the desk. "You said you had a long flight? From where?"

She rolled her eyes inwardly. *Small talk?* She didn't have time for this. "London."

He scratched his head. "Dr. Philipps said you'd been working abroad for six months, but I could have sworn it wasn't London."

She gave him a tight smile. "No, I've been living in Eritana."

"Eri—wha?"

"It's a small country in the Caucuses, north of Azerbaijan."

"And what were you doing there?"

"I was doing research on the properties of the minerals found in the Vaisjaani Nature Reserves," she said smoothly.

"Sounds, er, interesting."

She smirked. "Yes, it was fascinating."

"So why did you leave?"

"We ran out of funding," she said. It was close enough to the truth. Hopefully he didn't notice the white lie because she had a feeling that despite his hulking size, Ben Walker wasn't a dumb oaf.

"I see." He picked up a folder on his desk. "Well, I've read through the resume Dr. Philipps forwarded to me. He's done nothing but sing praises about you. But tell me: why would you want to be our Chief Geologist?"

Violet sighed and her shoulders sagged. This was an amazing opportunity. She would get to study blackstone, the hardest substance on Earth which could only be mined by dragon fire. Anyone in her field would have given their right arm for this and she had been flattered that her mentor, Dr. Scott Philipps, had chosen her as his replacement. But she wished the timing were better.

"Dr. Robichaux?"

"Right." She cleared her throat delicately. "Mr. Walker—"

"Ben, please."

"All right. Ben. This job would be excellent for my career. I've always been fascinated with the properties of blackstone ever since Dr. Philipps brought a sample to class. So, when he told me about this job a few weeks ago, I jumped at the chance. But I also need to be honest with you. Something came up, and I'm still waiting on another opportunity."

"And what's that?"

She cleared her throat. "I'm trying to secure funding to further my research back in Eritania. I've left a few things undone. I'm afraid I won't be able to accept any position at the moment." She stood up. "My flight was already booked, so I thought I'd come anyway. My apologies for wasting your time."

"Wait." Ben got to his feet and raised a hand. "I mean, please stay, Dr. Robichaux, and hear me out."

Huh? Curiosity pricked at her. "All right." She sat back down and crossed a leg over her knee.

"Dr. Philipps has been with us for almost twenty years now, and he's a well-respected part of our team. We're sad to see him go, but of course he deserves to retire. As you know the position is highly specialized, but aside from the skill and knowledge we also need someone who would fit in around here. With our people."

"Oh." He meant shifters, of course. She knew the prejudices they faced.

"I know Dr. Philipps really wants to get on with his retirement, and I hate to keep him here. So how about this: why don't you fill in temporarily until we can find someone else?"

"Really? You'd let me stay knowing I could leave any moment?"

"Why not? I'll give you a full six months' salary, plus housing and all the benefits if you can stay and help us with the transition. I mean who knows, you might like it here and decide to stay."

She highly doubted that but bit her tongue. A whole six months' salary for a few weeks of work? If she secured her funding for the year, that additional money could keep her going for another couple of months. Plus she could see them mine the blackstone. She would be stupid to refuse.

"That's very generous of you. Are you sure?"

"Oh, I'm very sure."

There was this ... glint in Ben Walker's eye. Was this some kind of trick?

Take it, the logical voice inside her said. The salary was pocket change to Lennox Corporation but would mean all the world to her.

"All right. That sounds reasonable. I also know a few people who might be a good fit." If she helped them find a replacement, she could leave Blackstone right away and have money to go back to Eritania. This was the perfect solution.

"I'll have HR draw up the papers. Are you staying in town?"

"At the Blackstone Hotel," she said.

Ben nodded. "You can keep staying there while you're here or move into one of our corporate apartments. Just let Janice in HR know what you'd like, and she'll take care of it for you."

"That sounds excellent."

"Can you start tomorrow?"

"Of course," she said.

"Good. You'll be working with our Chief Engineer, Nathan Caldwell. He works with Dr. Philipps closely." He paused. "Is that okay?"

She shrugged. If this Nathan Caldwell worked with Dr. Philipps, she was sure he would be a fine colleague. "That's fine."

Ben's face lit up. "Great."

She stood up. "If you don't mind, I'd like to get some rest."

"Of course. Just call if you need anything else. And, uh …" He looked at her outfit.

"Don't worry. I have some appropriate work clothes." She was used to digging in the dirt after all. But, since today was a formal interview, she wanted to look nice.

"Good. You'll be doing a lot of work inside the mines, so you should wear some sturdy shoes."

"I will. Thank you again, I'll see myself out." With a final nod, she pivoted on her heels and headed out the door.

As she walked to her car, Violet still couldn't believe what had happened. She was going to be working with blackstone of all things, making a generous salary, and she could walk away anytime she wanted? Maybe the Ben Walker wasn't as smart as he looked or there was something in the mountain air that was rotting his brain.

A scent in the air caught her attention. It was male, spicy, and smelled so good her knees buckled.

Mine!

"Stop!" She was glad no one was around. It must have been her imagination, or her hyper senses picking up the lingering scent. "He is *not* ours. Didn't you hear what he said?"

If her sense of smell was good, her hearing was even better.

Newsflash Ben: I don't want her either.

You think I want a mate?

I'm drowning in so much—

Jealous growls silenced her thoughts.

"You're being unreasonable." She yanked open the door of her rented car. "And I can't believe I'm even talking to you."

Violet slid into the front seat and shoved the key into the ignition. A deep breath escaped her lips.

"He's not interested. He's far too busy entertaining other women." The angry snarl was something she'd never heard before, especially not from her own mouth.

"No, we have to forget about him." She closed her eyes. "Remember why we're here. So we can go back. *Remember.*"

Her tiger quieted down as her own chest tightened with pain.

"Now, let's focus."

When she didn't hear any more protests, she turned the key and drove back to her hotel.

The Blackstone Wolf
Blackstone Mountain Book 4

Available now on Amazon!

OTHER BOOKS BY ALICIA MONTGOMERY

PARANORMAL SERIES:

The True Mates Series

Fated Mates

Blood Moon

Romancing the Alpha

Witch's Mate

Taming the Beast

Tempted by the Wolf

The Lone Wolf Defenders Series:

Killian's Secret

Loving Quinn

All for Connor

The Blackstone Mountain Series

The Blackstone Dragon Heir

The Blackstone Bad Dragon

The Blackstone Bear

CONTEMPORARY SERIES:

THE BILLIONAIRE HEIRS

Seducing the Billionaire's Daughter

Surrendering to the Billionaire's Son

THE COMBUSTION SERIES

Take Me There

Hearts on Fire

All of Me

THEIR GAME

Let the Games Begin

The Game is On

End Game

Printed in Dunstable, United Kingdom